The Ultimate Cure

Peter Harboe-Schmidt

The Ultimate Cure

To Toby

For the pursuit of our
dreams and the discovery
of our own true nature.

All the best for your
venture!

Yours,

Peter Harboe-Schmidt

2012.10.05

The Ultimate Cure

ISBN: 982-2-8399-0454-4

Jacket graphics: Michael Babel

Printed and bound in Germany by stm-media, Köthen

This novel is a work of fiction. Any references to real events and locations are intended only to give the fiction a sense of authenticity.

www.the-ultimate-cure.com

1

"Hang on ..." said the young man sitting on the edge of the pavement. One of his roller skates needed adjusting. He pushed a set of yellow sunglasses, almost the size of ski goggles, back on top of his head.

His two friends stood in the street. One was tall with a small goatee and a pierced eyebrow, long bleached hair sticking out underneath his helmet; the other was bare-chested with the thin strip of his black shorts showing above the waistline of his worn, low-slung jeans.

The air around the men was vibrating excitedly. On several previous occasions, they had postponed their attempt, usually because of some small annoying hitch that prevented them from going for the ultimate experience. Today the whole universe seemed to co-operate, setting the scene for a perfect morning. The sun had risen over the mountains, quickly heating up the humid earth. A handful of clouds moved unhurriedly across the Lausanne sky.

During the half-hour trip by metro and bus to one of the highest parts of the town, their impatience had almost turned into agony. Now they stood in front of the north entrance to the Olympic stadium and looked down the road with excitement. Red-leaved maple trees grew on the left side of the black asphalt that seemed to continue down through an endless flood of buildings. Slightly further on, the street dipped even more, making the town look like a miniature version of San Francisco.

In just five minutes, they would reach the harbour.

A simple framework set up to propel them into the outer spheres of freedom, requiring plenty of unrestrained speed. As travellers in a world with laws that knew no law, they would encounter traffic lights about a dozen times – adrenaline would be necessary to get them across the red ones. But then again, it was early on a Sunday morning in summer and very quiet; only occasionally did a car go by.

"That's it – let's go!" the man with the goggles shouted. He pulled the glasses back over his eyes and pushed a button on his wristwatch. A "Yeeaaah!" of endorsement came almost in unison from his two friends.

The skates made only a slight sound as they gathered speed on the dark, even surface. The young men had chosen to go by the east side of the stadium. The first sharp right turn went well, they were all in good control, making wide slalom-like turns without skidding.

After passing two green lights, they slowed down in front of 'Ms. Twenty-two', losing a few precious seconds as they did so. One of the steepest streets in town, the 'lady' had earned her nickname by promising lots of adventure. With a twenty-two percent gradient, the road seemed almost to disappear down into the lake; that alone made it a frozen and slippery nightmare for car drivers in winter. But the street was really a little piece of dreamland for the few who embraced gravity instead of fighting against it. This marked the start of serious fun.

Howling like a pack of wolves, freed from the captivity of daily life, the skaters thrust themselves on to the blackness of the newly laid asphalt that made perfect contact with their wheels. The sudden yells startled a terrier on a balcony, its wild barking fuelling their delighted screams as they took another two turns, nearly getting in one another's way on the narrow street.

A modern structure with bright blue windows flashed past, reflecting square images of the surroundings just before they crossed their first red light – luckily, there were no cars on the intersecting road.

It would take very little to end the adventure. An unexpected bump, however small, or even the tiniest pebble would be enough to toss them into a tree or through a shop window. Yet none of this seemed to worry them on their unstoppable journey.

The sweet and heady scent of freshly baked bread hit their nostrils and disappeared within a fraction of a second before they tore across another traffic light that had turned red. For a brief moment, no sound could be heard, except the wind singing in their ears and ruffling their hair.

Intoxicated by excitement, they crossed the Chauderon Bridge, standing high above the roads and buildings underneath. A bus was in front of them as they drifted by on the leftmost lane, shouting and making provocative gestures. Behind the windows, a few sleepy passengers glanced at the skaters with curiosity.

Further down the street, a powerful off-roader, impeccably clean from a recent car-wash, stood in front of the central train station. The driver, a newspaper in his hand, was on his way back to the car. He climbed inside, dropped the paper next to a cellophane-wrapped bouquet of flowers lying on the passenger seat and, with the engine making its comforting throaty roar, slowly manoeuvred the vehicle out of the parking space. After crossing the roundabout, he turned up the Avenue Louis Ruchonnet.

With the wrist of one hand resting loosely on the steering wheel, he turned on the radio and heard James Brown singing 'I feel good'. He cheerfully hummed along and turned up the volume.

At that same moment, the car found itself facing one of the three skaters head-on as they came out of a sharp turn. The driver froze, his vocal chords suddenly too paralysed by the abrupt change of scene to utter a sound. He automatically slammed his foot down on the brake and pulled the steering wheel hard to the right.

He lost control of the vehicle. It swayed dangerously from side to side as he counter-steered to avoid the skaters who were heading towards the side of the road. Blue smoke rose from the wheels and the car did a U-turn before skidding backwards across the street. For an instant, music from the car windows blended with the sound of squealing tyres. Still clasping the steering wheel in shock, the driver was now facing the direction he came from, his eyes wide open in fear. The skater with the naked torso managed to jump on to the pavement just in time to avoid a collision.

Seconds later, the car hit a lamp post by the side of the road in an explosion of crushed steel and shattered security glass.

The three young men slowed down hesitantly, taken aback by the new turn of events and the sudden silence that followed. The shirtless skater smiled quietly as he looked back over his shoulder. With a raised arm, he made a two-fingered victory salute. It was all turning out exactly the way he thought it would. Their downhill conquest was becoming anything but a runaway victory.

2

"When will your drugs go into human clinical trials?"
The analyst who asked the question looked quite young, perhaps less than thirty years of age. Like a tireless woodworm, steadily chewing through the material, he would not stop until all the knots had been found.

Opposite him, on the other side of a large oval cherry-wood table, Martin Rieder and Tanya Karnov found themselves in the midst of a barrage of questions following the presentation of their biotechnology start-up company to a small group of partners and analysts of a venture-capital firm.

Martin shifted in his seat.

"I suppose it'll take another year before the first clinical trials can begin," he replied.

No one in the room made any comment. Martin looked at Tanya, seeking her agreement. Their eyes met, but she remained silent.

One of the partners, his hair combed over a bald patch and wearing a blue bow tie with white dots, went in and out of the room, apparently trying to participate in two meetings simultaneously. Several times, he sat down only to repeat some of the questions that had already been answered.

Martin noticed that the other analyst, a stylishly-dressed woman with her long dark-blond hair pinned up, had been flicking through her notes for a while.

"You've listed many different cancers in your business plan," she said. The nasal tone of her voice made her sound quite formal.

"Even pancreatic cancer. Do you really think you can treat them all? What about the stage of the cancers?"

Tanya broke in.

"I personally think that today's cancer treatment has one fundamental problem."

She was soft-spoken, but everyone in the room listened.

"Tumours are classified and treated according to their location and appearance. Breast cancer, lung cancer, colon cancer and so on."

As she talked, her delicate and slightly nail-bitten fingers stabbed at the air to emphasize her words.

"Nature doesn't work that simply," she said. "I'm sure that's the reason for the slow progress in cancer therapy."

"That's a pretty bold statement, Ms Karnov."

Dr Kohler, the managing partner of Life Technology Ventures, spoke for the first time since the company presentation finished.

"You're saying that the classification and staging systems, which oncologists have been using for decades, are all wrong?"

Kohler's head was tilted slightly to the side and his eyes were emitting an almost disconcerting directness. The voice seemed to come from a place of deep experience.

Tanya tucked a lock of hair behind her ear.

"Maybe those old diagnostic paradigms are outdated. I mean, wouldn't it be better to understand what really happens inside the tumours, within each cancer cell, regardless of where they're located?"

"You could be right, but we prefer to leave revolutions to others, Dr Karnov," Kohler said. "The whole system is set up according to the old paradigms you're talking about. Many people want to keep it that way for the moment. That's our playing field."

Martin noticed the hint of a blush appearing on Tanya's face. He could tell she was holding back, keeping some comment or other to herself. The analysts seemed happy enough. Another knot, albeit a very slight one, in the wood.

The bow-tied partner sitting next to Kohler grunted briefly and took the opportunity to leave the room again. This time he did not return.

"So you're looking for ten million Swiss francs?" the woman analyst asked.

"We need that to get us past phase one, the first human safety trials, for the two protein-drug candidates we've shown you today," Martin replied.

His answer was written down without further comment.

The analyst had one more question on his list.

"How did you come up with the company name, *Attis Therapeutics?*"

"We wanted a name starting with an 'A' to get us at the front of the different directories," Martin said. "*Attis* for Advanced Therapeutic Tumour Intervention Solutions. It's also the name of a Greek god of fertility."

Kohler smiled.

"I like the name. *Attis*. Sounds like pharmaceuticals. Like Aventis, Novartis. Good choice."

Kohler always trusted his first impressions. These two scientists were quite outstanding. Martin was definitely a young entrepreneur with potential. The clarity of his presentation had been remarkable. Tanya knew her stuff and had not given his analysts a chance. She was an amazing researcher who would, if managed correctly, produce some real scientific wonders.

"You want to be king or to be rich?" Kohler asked abruptly.

The question caught Martin a little off-guard and he sensed that Kohler was using every second to assess them. An air of defiance came over Tanya's face as if either option were a personal offence.

Initially, Martin had wanted to believe in nothing but virtuous reasons for the start-up. What could be more noble than helping to cure cancer sufferers all over the world?

But the encounter with venture capitalists had struck a chord with an even deeper desire. The exclusive-looking offices. The big deals they all talked about. The pervading suggestion of a high return on investment.

The smell of burnt Porsche in people's footsteps.

Martin loved it.

There were many fine causes and they all made sense, but being truly honest to himself, he had to admit that the prospect of making a lot of money in this venture was what excited him most.

"I suppose we just want this company to succeed," Martin heard himself say. "It's really that simple. With whatever it takes to get there. The rest will follow." He tried to sound as relaxed and confident as possible.

Kohler remained quiet.

"We're both inventors of the patents and obviously want to be involved with their future," Tanya added.

She was not quite candid about the inventor part. Only her persistence had finally led them to their discoveries. Martin had been close to losing his equanimity on several occasions.

"You already have a private investor, right?" The woman analyst looked at Tanya.

"Yes."

"There is no name in the business plan. Who is it?"

Tanya hesitated for a moment. She glanced at the large unframed painting with squares in red and brown shades that covered most of the wall behind Kohler and his colleagues.

"Well ... our investor wishes to stay anonymous for the moment. We could tell you if you were willing to sign a secrecy agreement."

"Perhaps just to clarify things a little," Kohler intervened, looking from one analyst to the other. "As a matter of principle we do not sign confidentiality agreements at this stage. But to give you some comfort, I can tell you that Life Technology Ventures is a member of the European Venture Capital Association. We fully respect their guidelines on handling confidential information."

"We must have a secrecy agreement before we can tell you who it is," Tanya insisted.

A drawn-out silence seemed to indicate that the meeting would soon be over.

"Let's come back to that later," Kohler said. "You know, once we choose to work with a company, we want to be fully connected with the management and the other investors. With an umbilical cord, we like to say."

He paused for a second.

"The fact that you have been invited here to present is already quite a recognition of your work and the business opportunity it opens up. Only one in a hundred proposals makes it to this room. Your supporting *in vitro* data aren't very strong yet. Normally we would not go further at this point."

Kohler knew he was taking a risk. But if this worked, if these therapeutics could really kill human cancer stem cells effectively, then Tanya and Martin could hold the key to a potential cancer cure – a key with huge commercial potential.

"However, I'm going to make an exception," he said, "and put you through the review process with our experts. That could probably take a couple of weeks. Meanwhile, I'd appreciate it if you could send us all the new data you gather from now on."

3

On the way back to the parking lot, Martin and Tanya passed an exclusive-looking cafe. Under normal circumstances, it would never have crossed Martin's mind to enter such a place. This cafe was for business people and those who were well-dressed. Only a year ago, he fitted neither category.

Martin looked at Tanya and pointed towards the door with a raised eyebrow. They hesitated for a moment, then went in.

The interior of the café looked as if old-fashioned chairs, tables and paintings had been thrown in to create a deliberate mismatch. Trendy, but rather un-Swiss. Three stylishly-dressed people were standing at the counter, looking as though they were waiting for some famous person or other to show up.

Martin settled down in a comfortable green upholstered chair and made a somewhat nervous signal to the waiter. Tanya sat down opposite him and looked around.

The waiter finally came over. Thin as a rake, he stood sideways-on to them and summarized their orders in a tone of polite unfriendliness.

After the waiter had sidled off, Martin sat back and carefully removed his tie without undoing the knot. It was a perfect Windsor knot. Large, loose and triangular, it projected loads of self-confidence. His friend Tom had tied it for him when they had had their first meetings with venture capitalists – or VCs as everyone called them.

That was four months ago and he still kept that tie knotted. It was blue with a fine pattern of small white flowers. He thought of his father, a wine-grower with an estate in the hills above the town of Sion in the Valais region who had always told him not to waste time with people who wore ties. *How can anyone with a constricted blood flow to the brain be expected to come up with bright ideas?*

"That was actually a good meeting," Martin said cheerfully. "I could see us working with that chap Kohler. What was that expression he used? *Umbilical cord?*"

He started laughing.

Unlike Kohler, many of the other financial people had drained away Martin's boundless energy and drive. The search for money was still exciting, but it was starting to take its toll. He hoped it would soon come to an end.

"I don't know," Tanya replied. "We've been at it since April and no investor has bitten yet. Perhaps we need to change tactics."

The waiter arrived and noisily set down a tray with two apple juices.

"Change what?" Martin felt a slight hint of criticism in what she said.

"Perhaps we don't sell our project as well as we could. Both of us."

Martin took a long sip from his glass.

"Come on, Tanya. The presentation is already much better." He leaned back in the chair, hands clasped behind his neck, and studied the ceiling.

Tanya was not completely wrong. Several people had told him the same thing. To head up a start-up company as Chief Executive Officer, the CEO, you had to be a good salesman. That annoyed him somehow. In his mind, salespeople were always fairly superficial. Some even profoundly superficial.

"You know what the Latin word for selling is?"

Tanya shook her head.

"*Vendere.* Which also means to betray. Interesting isn't it?"

Of all salespeople, the telemarketers were the worst. Directly intruding into your private sphere without warning. And at the very bottom would be those telemarketers who phone round about dinnertime. Martin had developed a very effective remedy against that kind of incursion. *'Can you just hold the line?'* was his standard response. Then he would leave the receiver on the table next to his plate while he finished dinner. He was impressed by one telemarketer who had actually stayed on the line for the remainder of a *salade niçoise.*

That had led Martin to another conclusion: selling required a pretty strong dose of patience – and he really didn't have very much of that.

"Why not change things?" Tanya said.

"Right." Martin looked away.

"You *can* be little stubborn, you know."

"Don't ask me to be someone other than I am. I know what I am not."

An elegantly-dressed couple entered the café and were instantly recognized by the barman. It was hard to tell whether they were famous or not, but they certainly got a lot of attention.

Martin studied Tanya in her unease with the surroundings. Her dark eyebrows were like straight lines beneath her auburn shoulder-length hair. As far as one could see, she never wore make-up and her face was quite pale regardless of the season. She was thin – in times of stress, tending towards anorexic. The round face was the only hint that she was of East European descent. Five years ago, her parents had moved back to St. Petersburg.

A mobile phone rang. Several people reacted before Martin realized that it was his.

"*Quoi de neuf?*" A gentle, crisp voice said.

Broccaz rarely wasted time on small talk.

"How did the meeting go?"

Martin silently cursed the background music in the café and pressed the mobile phone harder to his ear, covering the other ear with his hand.

"I'm doing a debrief with Tanya right now," Martin said. "I think we did pretty well. The presentation was good. They seem to be interested, asking us for a pile of extra information. I believe we'll have an answer in a couple of weeks."

"Let's leave *believing* to the priests. We should start knowing instead."

Broccaz paused, letting the discomfort hang out a little on the phone line. "Okay, anything we can do to push this answer in a positive direction?"

"I imagine any positive news from the lab would help."

"Can I speak to Tanya for a minute?"

Martin handed the phone to her.

With a slightly uncomfortable look on her face and a vocabulary becoming ever more succinct, Tanya made a gesture to Martin, indicating that it was too noisy in the café. Still listening to what Broccaz was saying, she went outside.

Tanya had brought Broccaz on board, apparently through an association of amateur piano-players. If there was one thing that matched Tanya's scientific excellence, her piano playing would be it. Martin was convinced that she could have had an equally promising career in music.

Martin knew very little about Broccaz. He was unusually discreet, even by Swiss standards. From what he knew through Tanya, Broccaz had made a significant sum of money in private banking. He seemed to have a powerful network of contacts, stretching from bankers and lawyers to well-known industrialists and even politicians, but the small venture capital sphere was rather new to him.

Apparently, philanthropic reasons were also part of Broccaz's decision to invest in Attis Therapeutics. His mother had suffered from colorectal cancer and had undergone a great deal of radiotherapy over a pain-filled two-year period before she passed away. His father also had died from illness shortly after. That had all happened many years ago when Broccaz was still young.

His contradictory personality often puzzled Martin. On some days, Broccaz would appear gentle and compassionate, on others completely unemotional. That must have been the basis of his success, Martin had concluded. The ability to switch off on command, to leave your feelings thoroughly wrapped up in the glove compartment of your car before you get out and walk to the office.

As he waited for Tanya to come back, Martin drank his juice and watched the other clients being served. His thoughts went back to all the work that was piling up. It made him feel tired.

"I think our article will have to wait a bit," he said when she came back in, "we'll be terribly busy this week."

Tanya was working on a paper that they would submit to *Nature Cell Biology*. An acceptance by such a reputable journal would be a fantastic achievement and have a strong impact on a scientific career. Tanya was the main author of the paper and Martin was going to be listed as one of the collaborators of the work behind it. Once more, he had been lucky to get a free meal.

Tanya's face reddened. "The reviewers are getting impatient. I don't want to lose the opportunity to get that paper published."

Martin was getting annoyed. "Tanya, either we play this startup game together or we don't!" he said much too loudly. "You said it yourself. We need to sell the project better. We both have to be fully committed to make it succeed. It's like being pregnant.

You can't just be a little pregnant. We've made a commitment to Broccaz."

"An article in *Nature Cell Biology* would be very useful for convincing investors," Tanya argued. "And the new data."

"I have a vague feeling that it won't be enough," Martin said with some irony.

He realized that the road ahead was leading to another heavy workweek when he would not see much of Sarah, his girlfriend, even at the weekend. They had been in a relationship for three years now and he loved her more than ever, but he was seeing less and less of her.

He wanted to be with her, kiss her, and look deep into her amber-coloured eyes. To feel her soft hands caressing his back and his neck as they made love. He wanted to run off with her to the south of Spain – or Italy, which he liked even better. To go to Florence and experience the atmosphere of the Renaissance. He wanted to get bored with her on a rainy autumn afternoon and feel time going slowly by. And to tell her how much he loved her and to imagine what their children would look like.

Perhaps they would become one of those rare old couples who could still light a candle and spend the whole evening talking.

Or maybe, one day, her patience would just run out.

4

A broad beam of late-afternoon sunshine moved across the floor, gradually climbing on to the bed of the sparsely-equipped hospital room. As it touched his face, the warmth and the light woke him up. His head felt heavy and he struggled to open his eyes.

Where was he?

The powerful pain medication had drained his memory. Feeling dizzy, he squinted at the photo on the table next to his bed. Although he couldn't see it clearly, he knew it pictured his wife and four children playing on sledges in the snow. The photo that normally stood on his work-desk in the library at home.

His scalp was bandaged and his left leg was in plaster all the way from foot to hip. As he anxiously turned his head, a horrendous throb of unbearable pain shot up inside his brain. He slowly moved his head back, letting his tired eyes do the exploring as far as they could. A small television set tilted downwards towards him from underneath the ceiling and a dozen fresh roses were arranged in a tall vase on the window-sill.

What was all this?

The medication drip and the transparent tube protruding from his arm certainly were genuine enough and the drip bottle looked empty. The pain started coming in waves all through his body, lapping at the shores of his nervous system. At first, hardly noticeable, like small ripples, then with increasing force. The pain cleared his mind, but the rest of his body remained uncooperative.

Now he remembered. The accident. Skidding towards the lamp post next to the road where everything turned black. It was such a fine morning and then, in a moment of slight inattention, a couple of insane skaters came and shattered it all. He recalled the last frightening moments after he lost control of his car. Those few seconds were a jumble of pictures from the past and the present.

'Will it hold?' was the last thought he remembered.

Now he knew it had. He had survived. Life had held up.

Those boys. It made him seethe with rage to think of them. Going on the middle of the road! What did these bloody boys think traffic rules were meant for? What kind of parent would bring up children like that?

With increasing irritation and pain, he reached up and pushed the button over his bed to call the nurse. He looked out the window and noticed that a bird, landing on a branch, began to sing eagerly. It made him feel imprisoned inside his body.

A nurse entered the room.

"How can I help you, Mr Menarti?" she said with a hint of empathy and a Swiss-German accent.

"My head is starting to hurt … really badly," he replied, noticing that his speech was slurred.

"I'll get you a new bottle for the drip – just need to take your blood pressure before that." She strapped a cuff round his arm and started pumping air into it.

"What happened to my body?" he said, feeling a bit foolish.

"Your car hit a lamp post. Without the airbags, things would have been much worse."

"And?"

"I was told that you have a moderate traumatic brain injury. Your skull has a slight fracture, probably from hitting the roof of the car or the window frame."

"And the plaster?" Menarti turned his eyes.

"You have two fractures on your thigh bone and a broken ankle. We took an X-ray earlier. The good news is that you don't have any injuries to your spinal cord."

"Great," he said with a sigh.

She was studying the pressure gauge. "Blood pressure looks fine. Anything else I can do for you?"

"Just get that pain medication going." He closed his eyes for a few seconds and said, "also, I … feel like vomiting."

"Unfortunately I am not allowed to give you any anti-emetics to stop your nausea, but let me get you something else."

She pulled out a bucket from underneath the bed and the moment she placed it on a tray-table next to the bed, Menarti's stomach was ready to revolt. He jerked his head towards the edge of the bed. An excruciating pain shot up through his body.

"Don't do that!" she said sharply, slowly rolling him over. "You should avoid sudden movements. It's not good for your head."

She held him until his stomach was empty. Then she wiped his mouth and helped him back on to the pillow.

"Now we'll take care of your pain." She went out to get a new drip bottle.

When she came back, he felt a bit better but the pain was still bad.

"So what about this brain injury?" he asked.

"I don't know much yet." She hooked up the bottle. "The doctor will come by to see you this morning," she said, opening the drip tube valves.

It did not take long before the medication brought him some relief. The nurse said that they were going to do a CT scan on him later. Just to be sure that none of his internal organs were damaged.

"How long do I have to stay here?"

"With this type of head injury, we usually keep people two-three days. During that time we'll find out if you need to stay longer."

"That long?"

"You were unconscious for three hours. Even though you seem to be making good progress, we want to keep you under observation."

"Life can be a pain," he said, his cheeks drained of all their colour. "Whenever you let down your guard, someone comes along and wants to blow the whole thing apart."

"It could be worse. You had a solid car, I heard."

Menarti did not even dare to ask what had happened to the car. He closed his eyes.

"Of course. Things could always be much worse ..."

As she went out of the room, leaving him a bit light-headed from the painkillers, he had a new and strange sensation that good fortune was about to come in his direction.

He promised himself that he was going to find them, those wild boys. As soon as he got out. By God he was going to find them.

5

It was a very early September morning when the high-pitched beep of an alarm clock woke Martin up, his eyes ever more aching from the accumulation of too little sleep and too many long workdays. Sarah mumbled something and turned over to the other side of the bed to continue her snooze.

He picked up the laptop and rushed into the kitchen. An endless to-do list was waiting impatiently for him. After a quick breakfast, he opened the computer on the small table and started working on a new operational plan, one that had been requested by a new potential investor from Munich.

Martin spent the morning producing a first rough draft of the plan. It was far from good and much more time-consuming than he had thought. At this rate, they would hardly be able to hand over anything decent to the VCs this week. Let alone the document on the patent environment, which he had planned to do tomorrow.

His tired brain felt like a wrung-out dishcloth as he left the flat. He was happy to let Tanya have a look at the document. Due to time pressure, they had decided to split the task. Tanya was working from home today to concentrate on various scientific reports, while Martin was going to take care of the lab.

Fifteen minutes later, the bustling noise of activity greeted him through the lab corridor. Satisfied, Martin went straight into his office and turned on the PC. He clicked on the Internet to have a quick glance at the biotech news. A blank screen told him that the Internet connection was down. He tried several times, but in vain. No deals; no milestone payments; no new start-ups; no discoveries. His lifeline to the world had been cut off. He came close to yelling in frustration and cursed himself for not e-mailing the documents to Tanya from home. He wondered how he was going to get the draft operational plan to her.

Come on, computer, unblock yourself!

His clenched fist hit the keyboard forcefully and resolutely, sending one of the plastic keys flying across the desk. He was struggling to hold back an overwhelming primeval desire to inflict further damage to the hardware when Fabienne, one of the lab technicians, came into the office.

He looked at her, slightly embarrassed.

"That bastard 'Return'-key on my keyboard decided to do a runner," he said with a laugh of wrathful irony and bent down underneath the table to inspect the floor.

"What's up?" he said from below. The key was nowhere to be seen.

"I can come back …"

"No, no … it's fine. It must be down here somewhere."

Martin sat up, his hair a little tangled. "Tell me."

"We have the final results," she said, looking slightly uncomfortable. "From the cancer cell culture test."

Tanya had set up an experiment to see if their drug, apart from acting on cancer stem cells, would also have an effect on various other cancer cell lines.

Fabienne put her black notebook on his desk and went over the results while Martin listened in silence. As she spoke, he became increasingly pale.

"Hang on a second …" he interrupted her, "this just can't be true, Fabienne!"

"I know …"

"Our protein-drug *stimulates* cancer cell growth!"

Not good news for an alleged cancer cure.

Martin suddenly had a terrible sinking feeling in the pit of his stomach. What was going on? He thought of all the hours they had worked in the lab – only to get this result. That first molecule was supposed to turn into a drug with blockbuster commercial potential. This result could blow it all apart.

Martin was gasping for breath. He tried hard to steady his nerves. The tiredness disappeared instantly. Something had to be wrong and he was going to find out what.

He ran into the laboratory.

The state of the lab could best be described as slightly worse than its usual state of chaos. Glassware, chemicals, test-tube racks and pipettes were spread across the workbenches along with paper notes and scientific magazines. Loud music came from a radio in the corner.

Martin ran over to the radio and pulled out the plug.

"HELLO. CAN YOU ALL HEAR ME?" He shouted with exaggerated loudness in the little room.

The three lab technicians stared silently at him in surprise from their workplaces. No one dared move.

"As of today, I want everyone in this lab to start behaving like professionals, okay? This is not a school playground, all right? We're supposed to be a business."

Martin tried as hard as he could to control himself.

"We may get big investor money in soon. That means no more mess, no more pop music while at work! You read me?"

They all nodded and slowly returned to their workplaces.

Martin demonstratively pushed aside everything that was stacked in front of Fabienne's desk. Something was wrong with the experiment and he was fully determined to find out what it was. He started to grill her extra hard on every single procedure of the previous week's experiments.

Fabienne's stuttering explanations and behaviour made him feel irritated. She was so damn insecure. Why was he the only one who had to do all the pushing and the thinking? Didn't he have enough hassle to deal with? The responsibility for it all, the people, the investors. And the company's bank account that was shrinking all too fast. Of the five hundred thousand Swiss francs from Broccaz, less than half was still left, just enough to keep them going for another four to five months. It was going to be awfully tight.

At midday, Martin felt his stomach churning unpleasantly. He ran over to the local bakery and bought two sandwiches, wolfing them down on the way back to the lab.

When he came back, the Internet was up and running again and he suddenly remembered the document he had to send to Tanya. How could he be so forgetful? There was just too much right now. Much too much.

His thoughts were all over the place and he tried hard to concentrate on the most urgent problems. All e-mails would have to wait. The issue with the drug was the most critical – it could mean the end of Attis Therapeutics. They had to solve it now. Martin had a long talk with Tanya on the phone. She suggested checking the replication rates of the cancer cells and comparing them with the data given by the supplier.

Late in the afternoon, Fabienne found the first signs that the cancer cells were dividing at a much slower rate than they were supposed to. That would most likely mean one thing: contamination of the cells, probably a virus that could interfere with the complex DNA replication machinery of the cell. It turned out that Fabienne had not tested the cells for infections beforehand.

"Everything is at stake right now and we behave like stupid amateurs!" Martin sneered. "Don't you understand? We need good and solid data now to survive. It'll take us days to find out what went wrong."

Fabienne held up her note pad.

"It has to be mycoplasma. Look, the pH-values didn't change at all," she said.

"Fine. Great." Martin was trying hard to control himself. He shook his head several times. "I don't care if our cell lines are infected with mycoplasma, bacteria … or friggin' *measles* for that sake."

He moved forward and lowered his face so that it was just in front of Fabienne's. "You all think you can just keep on doing experiments until hell freezes over! What I care about is that we don't know how the cells became infected and that we have lost several weeks of work."

Fabienne was on the brink of tears.

"I'm sorry," she said.

"What do you think would happen if the investors we're trying to get on board could see this?"

She shrugged.

"These things scare them," Martin said, "I can guarantee you that."

There had been too many of those bad days lately, causing several delays in the time plan.

Martin needed fresh air. He was about to take off his lab coat when the phone on his desk rang. He picked up the receiver.

"Hi sweetheart. It's me."

Martin tried hard to swallow away his frustrations.

"Sarah … oh … glad to hear it's you. How was your day?"

"Fine. I miss you," she said with a soft voice gradually becoming firmer. "Did you have time to hand over my drawings to Mr Falcroft in Rolle?"

Christl! How could he have forgotten that?

"Hum … not yet," Martin said, trying to sound as if everything was under control. "Honey, it's been a pretty crazy day at the lab. I was planning to go later this afternoon and–"

"Martin, you told me you would go during your lunch break!" Sarah interrupted.

"Yes, yes. You know what? I'll just drop everything to–"

"I was up until two in the morning working on it and you just forgot?!" Sarah snapped.

"Listen, Sarah, I really had a lot of issues today."

"I could have gone over to him myself. It's almost six now! Don't you get it? I have to give him the drawings today before he leaves for Scotland. I promised him and you promised me."

"I'm sorry," Martin said, knowing it would be unwise to argue.

Sarah let out a deep sigh.

"When you haven't got the time, don't promise this kind of thing to me. The drawings are in your car. What am I going to do now?"

Martin had wanted so badly to do her a favour; to make up for all those late evenings and weekends and yet he had forgotten everything.

"Honestly Sarah, I'm sorry. He'll get your drawings in less than an hour." Martin looked at his watch, set ten minutes ahead of time.

"Be nice to Mr Falcroft, he's a good friend of my boss."

"Right. I'll come straight home afterwards and it'll just be the two of us enjoying the rest of the evening together."

"I'll probably be asleep by then …"

"Maybe I'll wake you up."

"Maybe you can't."

"Don't bet on it!"

6

Martin left the motorway at the *Rolle* exit. The nagging feeling of wasting precious time had turned into anger against himself. How could he yell at people for not trying hard enough, when he himself took time off for an escapade like this? We proudly present the CEO of Attis Therapeutics, on his way to deliver an urgent garden plan to a deer-stalking, loch-fishing Scotsman.

Ok, point taken, he would make the encounter a short one. Polite hellos, a bit of small talk, hand over the drawings, no drink, thanks and good-bye. He could be back in Lausanne quite soon and the whole thing would have taken him no more than an hour. Perhaps this could even end the day on a productive note.

The road wound upwards through the vineyards of *Mont-sur-Rolle*. The scorching summer had prematurely ripened the yellow-green grapes. They were small but full and would be ready for harvesting any day now. The wine-growers would turn them into those light and slightly sparkling white wines that were very refreshing. But they were nothing compared to the wines of the *Valais*, so full of character, Martin thought as he drove past the fields with the car windows open. The view over the lake was unhindered and spectacular. A few boats were scattered across the water.

The small road ended in a T-junction. In front was an old, tall ivy-covered stone wall. There was no visible entrance, so Martin followed the whole length of the wall then turned right at the corner. He drove uphill, turned right again at another corner and finally found the way in through a large open metal gate. A letter-box on the wall next to the gate confirmed that Martin had found his destination.

He drove through a short alley leading to the house. As soon as he parked the car in the gravel-covered courtyard, a black retriever and a small brown cocker spaniel came bounding out towards him. The barking dogs started running round him as if rejoicing in their new prey.

A garden door next to the house opened and a firm voice resounded through the courtyard.

"*Popper, Finch.* Come here. *Finch!* Leave that young man alone."

Gavin Falcroft was wearing blue overalls partly covered in cement. He was older than his voice seemed to indicate, probably in his mid-sixties, his white hair in a crew-cut.

The cocker spaniel took one last quick sniff at Martin's trouser leg and then hurried up to its master who led the dogs to the front door and pushed them inside.

"How do you do, I'm Martin Rieder, Sarah Aguirre's *fiancé.*"

A bit intimidated by Gavin's charismatic allure, Martin shook the large fleshy hand.

"Well, then. Glad to meet you. I'm Gavin. Come on in."

Martin opened the car boot and took out the large plastic cylinder that contained Sarah's drawings.

"Here, I think this is what you've been waiting for."

"You can say that again. Let's go into the garden for a minute and have a look at them."

Gavin beckoned Martin through a small garden door and they walked around the house. It seemed like a cross between an English manor and an Italian *rustico*. Solid was the best word to describe it. Hundreds of tons of stone and cement – as if it were a direct result of Gavin's way of life. Martin wondered what things looked like inside.

Gavin walked straight to a large square teak table on the terrace.

"Care for some barley water?"

"I'm afraid that I have to leave pretty soon."

Martin noticed how his words for some reason were completely devoid of conviction. Apparently, Gavin did as well.

"Now, young man. No one has ever refused to at least *try* my barley water." Gavin's penetrating blue eyes burned with determination below the grey bushy eyebrows.

Be nice to Mr Falcroft, Sarah's voice echoed inside Martin's head.

"Well, I suppose one glass would be all right. A quick one."

"Good. You know, that stuff has some interesting health benefits. Gives the old liver a bit of a rest. And it's supposed to clear up the complexion and prevent wrinkles."

Martin glanced at the lake. "You have a fantastic garden. What a view!"

"*Where the lawns are wide and the minds are narrow,* as good old Hemingway used to say," Gavin said with a wry smile.

The vast garden stood out in all its simplicity like an oasis in the midst of the ruler-straight rows of vines on all sides. Even the tall pine trees at the end of the garden did not restrict the view over the lake and the Alps. The snow-covered Mont Blanc was now clearly visible after the fine mist over the lake had disappeared. There was a smell of pine-needles and grass and a couple of naked stumps revealed that some trees had recently been cut down. A small annex house was covered with a tarpaulin.

"You're renovating?" Martin said, pointing to the annex.

Gavin nodded.

"Remember the horrible storm we had two months ago?"

Martin certainly did. Many boats in the harbours around the lake had been severely damaged by the hurricane-force winds.

"Two of the tallest trees in the garden fell over. One of them was a tall poplar. It fell right on top of the old lodge. I'll never forget the sound it made … like someone dumping a huge load of gravel in the garden. The tree almost cut the house in two. It struck with unbelievable force."

Gavin let out a long sigh of frustration.

"This place always seems to keep me busy. It was a terrible mess. We've had a very hectic summer since then. I even missed out on this year's Tattoo at the Edinburgh Festival."

"And now you want to re-do the garden?"

"Yes, with Sarah's help. I don't know how we're going to get rid of those big trees. Sarah said that the Swiss authorities could create a lot of bother."

"There are stories about people going to jail for cutting down trees without permission," Martin said.

"You folks really do have a sense of justice," Gavin grinned.

He opened the cylinder, unfolded the drawings excitedly and laid them out the table next to the jug. Without a word, he studied the many circles, with their different colours and sizes. There was also a large blue rectangle, probably a swimming pool.

"Lindsey – that's my wife – she'll go crazy when she sees this. She is a complete garden nutcase who hates wilderness and insists on nice paths with benches and lots of new plants. I'm more concerned about getting that lodge rebuilt."

Martin took a quick glance at his watch. It was seven already, but his growing fascination for Gavin was overriding anything else. He just could not get himself to leave.

"Tell me what you do for a living," Gavin said.

"I'm a molecular biologist and I work for my own start-up company."

"Interesting. What's the start-up about?"

"We're developing new cancer medications, then we license them to big pharmaceutical companies once we have the initial proof that they work on human beings." Martin tried to use as simple words as possible.

Gavin had noticed how rapidly the region was gaining importance in the life science business area. The sheer number of new interesting start-ups in the area left little room for doubt.

"I know the field a bit. I had my own company with veterinary products back in Scotland. We were selling instruments and diagnostics for farm animals. Pigs, poultry, cattle, sheep. Even horses."

"And now?" Martin asked.

"Sold it to a big German company a while ago."

"Why?"

"Well, there are moments in life where professional and personal circumstances create a perfect opportunity for you. It doesn't happen often. Perhaps once or twice in a lifetime. You need to see it happening and be ready to grab the opportunity. It could be the only one you'll ever get."

"And this was the one?"

"My daughter ran into a Swiss laddie from Geneva and they got married. My wife has always been very close to our wee girl so we decided to move to Switzerland. The weather here is much better than in Oban. Mind you, the weather *anywhere* else in the world is better than in Oban."

"You don't miss your company?"

"I certainly do. Often. It was like my third baby – actually my wife called it my first!" Gavin's eyes widened. "I started it with a loan from my father. Over the years it became a nice profitable business and we began to develop our own products."

"But you sold it."

"Yep. Made a wee bit of money out of it."

A wee bit of money! Martin thought. *This place must be worth a fortune.*

"It was hard for me to sell the company. Much tougher than you think. I felt personally responsible for my employees and their families. It's different today. Entrepreneurs today just play with venture capital fun-money. The name of the game is to get the company sold, make money fast. People don't matter."

Gavin cleared his throat.

"You know, at that time, I had to carry the risk myself. High-risk investors were just not around then. And believe me, I think that created better entrepreneurs with a stronger sense of ownership. If you failed, you lost your money and sometimes your house as well."

Martin couldn't but feel impressed, but he did not entirely agree.

"I think biotech is one of the few industries where you cannot do without venture capital at some point," he said. "The risks and the investment needs are very high."

"You're probably right," Gavin said, "but I could never work with these people. Smart Alecs with fancy PhDs, MDs and MBAs, thinking they know how to run businesses. For most of them, *profit* is something they've only seen on television."

"Gavin … Gavin … easy now," a crisp female voice suddenly said behind them.

They turned round. A middle-aged woman and a man in his mid-thirties came through the open glass door on to the terrace.

"My wife, Lindsey and my son, Lorne," Gavin said.

They shook hands.

"Martin is Sarah's fiancé. He brought the garden drawings over."

"Oh, *that* Martin," she said instantly. "Do you know how lucky you are, young man? Sarah is such an adorable girl. What a pity she couldn't come with you."

Lindsey was not good-looking in any traditional sense. She was rather plump, an impression reinforced by her loose-fitting and garishly-coloured floral dress. Her true beauty came in all of its force from a smile that lay somewhere deep inside her. It surfaced as a permanent ray of sunshine in her eyes and on her lips.

"Oh my, Gavin has already found another volunteer for his noxious home brew," she said and looked eagerly at the garden drawings and plant pictures for a brief moment.

"I want lots of topiary shrubs," she said, as though in a dream. "Look at that yellow yew tree bush. Isn't it just stunning? It's clipped into a perfect sphere!"

Lorne was surprisingly handsome. His long darkish-fair hair was slightly curled and pulled back into a short ponytail. He was slim, dressed in dark clothes and he wore leather bands on both wrists. Martin looked at him enviously as his handshake was returned somewhere close to the lower end of the firmness scale. *Lucky you, to have a father like Gavin.*

"My boy was a student for two years at Glasgow University. Mathematical category theory to be exact."

"I don't know all that much about ... *category theory?*" Martin looked questioningly at Lorne.

"It's to do with objects and the abstract relations between them. You strip away unnecessary details and get to the essence of things. Suddenly you realize that many objects are actually quite similar," Lorne explained.

"But instead of finishing a great education as one of the brightest students the Mathematics Department had seen in a decade, he chose to leave," Gavin interrupted.

"I *had* to stop," Lorne corrected.

"Aye. Then go squandering about half a life, trying to figure out who he is." Gavin's face reddened in frustration and he turned his face towards Martin. "Call it global drifting if you will."

Gavin could not hide his disappointment at the outcome of Lorne's short academic career. "I *really* hope you find out what you want by the time you're forty, son."

"That's enough Gavin! At least Lorne takes the time to be with his family and friends," Lindsey said. "Sometimes I wish you had done more of that in *your* younger days."

The sudden exposed privacy of strangers made Martin feel uncomfortable. He was fascinated by Gavin and regretted that Lindsey and Lorne had turned up.

"My father and I see the world through two different lenses," Lorne said calmly. The vague and slightly distant expression on his face had not changed. "I love him even though we don't have all that much in common."

"Except that you eat my croissants every morning," Gavin said, clearly annoyed. "And after that you sit for hours reading and meditating in your room. Living your life on some other-worldly planet."

"Now you two, stop arguing," Lindsey said, with that seemingly-permanent smile on her face. "Would you like a bite to eat Martin? I've got some fresh olives and could make some *bruschette*."

Martin thanked her politely and said that he would have to leave because he had an appointment.

"At any rate, thanks for bringing the drawings," Gavin said. "I really enjoyed meeting you. Hope we can catch up again. Why don't you and Sarah come over for dinner some time?"

"We'd be delighted," Martin said. He was certain that Gavin could be a great source of advice for future dealings with investors. Perhaps he could even become a friend.

"I'm off to Scotland tomorrow," Gavin said. "I'll give you a shout once I'm back."

On the way home in the Clio, Martin mulled over the countless things he had to do. It was close to eight in the evening. The pile of work, which had probably swollen even more during the past couple of hours, would by now have reached epic proportions. He had not seen much of Sarah lately and wanted to have dinner with her.

The traffic on the motorway was unusually heavy and Martin became more and more tense. He hated traffic jams. It brought out the worst in him. And the claustrophobia.

His hands were sweating heavily.

The traffic started to slow down. Something was definitely wrong, probably an accident ahead. This part of the motorway was as straight as anything, but every single day some lunatic or other, bored to tears, would attempt to turn it into the Monte Carlo Circuit.

Where were the Swiss police, so famous for appearing out of nowhere as soon as an accident occurred?

Martin could see nothing but cars and felt trapped. Primitive alarm mechanisms made his pulse race and he began to feel a pain in his chest. He had felt anxiety in similar situations, but today was much worse. More like panic.

He was struck by a sudden urge to hit the accelerator, run over the cars and get into a nearby field, far away from the constriction.

To breathe freely again.

Martin could think of nothing else as he stared into the break lights of the cars in front, trying to control himself.

After another ten painful minutes of stop-go driving, a car bumped into his Clio from behind. The culprit was a Honda with a young man in the driver's seat.

Martin threw the door open, jumped out of the car and ran back to the Honda.

They all came out. Words that Martin had not used since high school thundered over the car roofs. Anxiety had turned into anger and it had spotted a victim. Wide-open eyes and mouths could be seen everywhere.

The young driver, completely gobsmacked in his seat, could only muster a few deprecatory gestures while Martin continued yelling about the infinite stupidity of people causing accidents at speeds of five kilometres per hour. Then the lad seemed to regain his composure after the bollocking and backed up his car in order to inspect the damage.

The bumper on Martin's car had hardly any visible scratches on the paint-work. In front, the other cars began to move again, providing some space for Martin to think more clearly. Without a word, he got back into his Clio, trying to control his anger and sense of foolishness. His hands were still trembling from the incident.

The traffic started flowing more smoothly again and the two lanes divided in accordance with the road markings. Martin took the right lane, then immediately regretted his decision when he saw a dozen policemen in bright-green fluorescent jackets.

Martin was waved over. *What was this now*?

A policeman spoke through the open window of the Clio. "Sir, we're doing a poll, a survey if you like. I have a questionnaire here. Would you be kind enough to fill it out for us?"

"What? Right here?" Martin said, as he wiped the sweat from his brow.

"No, when you get back home."

"What's it about?"

"Your driving habits."

"You're kidding. Right?"

"No Sir."

"A poll about my driving habits in a traffic jam that you just created?"

"No. About your general driving habits. Whether you drive to work, shopping, sports. What kind of parking space you use. Things like that ..."

Martin swallowed hard – twice – in an attempt to keep calm.

"I ... I've been waiting almost one hour on the road to fill in a questionnaire? And ... and now you're asking me about my *driving habits*? Why the hell didn't you just send me the bloody questionnaire?"

"Sir, may I suggest that you take things just a little easier? You could end up waiting much longer ... if you see what I mean."

Martin took a long, deep breath and was waved through. He looked at his watch. Almost nine p.m. – too late to phone Sarah; she would have gone to bed early, given the little sleep she had had last night. But not phoning her would be just as bad.

Thank God for SMS.

When Martin arrived in the rue St-Augustin, he found a parking place not too far from the flat. His legs felt heavy during the walk up the staircase. There was no lift in this old building and he lived in an attic on the fourth floor. His eyes were burning with fatigue.

Sarah was in a deep sleep when Martin entered their bedroom. He watched her face for a little while and removed a book lying open next to her on the pillow. He loved her beautiful face – especially now, when it had that blissful look that all sleeping people have. He wondered why all relaxed faces looked happy. Was that the truly natural state for all human beings to be in?

He looked closely at Sarah's long, beautiful, jet-black hair, her dark eyelashes that curled upwards. For several minutes, all he did was look at her. Her olive-tanned skin seemed almost black against the bright white pillow. He wished that she could have seen the Falcrofts' reaction when they got her drawings.

He decided not to wake her up and switched off the light.

Some paella was waiting for him in the fridge. He took it out and ate it straight from the pan.

What a day.

He uncorked a bottle of *grappa*, poured some into a glass and drank it quickly. He filled a second glass and went into the bathroom. He sat down in the bath tub and turned on the hot and cold taps, mixing a large dose of bubble bath with the gushing water.

A soft, soothing glow ran all through his body and relaxed his mind. Everything began to appear lighter. Then he had the same thought that always made him smile whenever he took a bath. It was his friend Tom's eloquent version of the Archimedes Principle.

When a body is fully submerged in a still fluid, a telephone starts ringing.

Martin had a quiet laugh to himself.

Nothing – but nothing – would get him out of *this* bath for the next half-hour.

7

The airport was surprisingly calm.

Greatly encumbered by the weight of his suitcase, Martin swore under his breath. He should have brought one that was easier to carry. Or at least one with wheels. This flight was far too important to miss and he ran as fast as he possibly could to reach the right desk in time.

He stopped for a moment and bent forward, one hand on his thigh and panted for breath. Where were the check-in desks?

Go straight to the gate then.

He looked up at the display screen showing all the departing flights. But to his disappointment there was no gate number indicated – that particular information field was still blank. The number should have been announced by now ...

There was something completely wrong here.

He thought he'd better check the time of his flight and pulled out the plane ticket from his coat pocket – but all he could see was a blank field. In despair, he tried to remember where he was going. No place-name came to mind.

What kind of ticket was this anyway? All tickets have a destination written somewhere, don't they?

Martin suddenly felt anxiety coursing through his body. It had a shrill ringing sound to it. He knew that sound – he'd heard it so many times before.

There it was again.

From far away, he heard Sarah's voice shouting.

"Please, Martin! Go get it! I really need to sleep."

Martin opened one eye and saw a glass floating upside down in the bath-water. Someone was ringing the doorbell. Martin jumped out of the bath, his heart pounding. He wrapped a towel around his waist and rushed through the flat, gradually realizing who – the one and only person – could possibly come by at this time of the evening. It had to be the master of proverbs, his friend through thick and thin.

Tom's mouth seemed to be buried even deeper than usually in the fleshy cheeks of a boyish and slightly apologetic face. Dressed in a dark T-shirt and shorts, his big sturdy body filled most of the doorway.

Martin realized that it was over three months since he had seen him. But with Tom, you could always expect the unexpected. He was everything that Martin was not. Unfocused, unpredictable and completely non-career-minded. Yet he was very conscious about what other people thought of him. Especially when those people were of the opposite sex.

"Coo-ee!" Tom smiled, revealing his gleaming-white front teeth. He pulled at Martin's towel. "Hope I didn't interrupt you guys in anything that I'm too old to do!" he continued with a loud laugh.

"Ssshhh, be quiet … Sarah's sleeping. What's up?"

"Locked myself out of my flat," Tom said in a thin, helpless voice while he turned the palms of his hands upwards. "I'm glad that I let you keep my spare key."

Martin often wondered why he liked Tom so much. Anyone who had a relationship with Tom, however close, would always be dragged into trouble or at least some kind of fire-fighting emergency. It was as unavoidable as pocket-fluff.

Martin would never forget that evening many years ago when they had watched *The Party*, starring Peter Sellers. What else could one do afterwards except test how the old street fountain around the corner would react to two full bottles of dish-washing liquid? After observing the fountain for half an hour without anything happening, he and Tom had gone home disappointed. Trouble came the next day when the police went looking for the culprits who had created the foam-covered monument that a witty journalist later touted to be by far the cleanest in the whole of Switzerland.

Not being caught after the implementation of Tom's wacky ideas was rather an exception. As a child, Martin would take whatever punishment his father deemed appropriate. It was the natural outcome of any wrongdoing; you had to pay and then the slate was wiped clean. It was the kind of fairness that the entire cosmos was founded on.

"Good to see the man himself for real," Tom said while Martin unhooked a key with Tom's name on it from a rack hanging on the wall next to the front door. "I almost forgot what you looked like!"

Tom observed Martin from the doorway.

"Hey, is that a beer belly in the making or are you just pregnant?"

He reached out to pat Martin's stomach with a flat hand.

Martin had put on four or five kilos over the past few months. The stress and lack of physical exercise had left their mark.

Tom looked up. "Okay ... tell me, what on earth are you up to? You're never home. Not even at weekends."

"I don't want to be rude, but I really need to get to bed." Martin grabbed Tom's arm and looked at the wristwatch. "It's almost eleven o'clock and I'm knackered."

"And what happens with your good old friend?"

"Listen. Another–"

"Not before you have one of these ..."

In one swift movement, Tom pulled out two bottles of Tuborg from apparently nowhere. "Got them in a pub on the way over.

And I warn you. I'll drink them both myself and pee on your doormat if you don't let me in."

Tom did most of the talking as they sat on the tiny balcony with a view over the thousand sparkling lights that came from the town of Evian on the other side of the lake. The main topic was the difficulty he had in finding a stable girlfriend. For some reason his relationships never lasted very long; four months was his, as yet unbeaten, record. His latest girl was from the Geneva upper crust. Given the exorbitant maintenance costs, Tom swore never ever to touch what he called a 'porcelain babe' again. Martin suspected that an integral part of the explanation was that the poor girl had finally succumbed to an overdose of humour.

"Sometimes I wonder if I should go gay," Tom said with a thin chuckle. It was melancholic at first but then became heavier and finally turned into a hearty laugh. For little or no reason, Tom could start laughing and it was always highly contagious. Too tired to resist, Martin joined his laughter. Tom's problems rarely lasted for very long. He never took them seriously. His life was like water, always flowing over the sharpest of rocks in an apparently calm manner.

"Enough about me. How's Sarah? Is she okay with you spending all that time on the start-up?"

Martin felt some of his energy coming back.

"She knows that I have to do it. This could be something really big, you know."

"You already told me, but tell me again: what kind of wild things are you brewing in the labs these days?"

Tom knew exactly when to put on that naïve, and really quite charming, expression he mastered so well. "I know it's something to do with cancer. But please, spare me too much fancy biology talk."

Martin bent down and picked up a yellow leaf from the floor of the balcony. "What's this?" he asked, holding it by the stem towards the light coming from the living room.

"Well, I see a withered leaf. I think it's an oak-leaf, although I wouldn't eat my hat if I were wrong".

"The ancient Greek poets," Martin said as he twisted the leaf from side to side, "described the falling of leaves from trees in autumn in one word: *Apoptosis*".

"A-pop-to-sis?" Tom repeated very slowly. "Bear with me Martin. In the evolution of mankind, my ancestors got stuck in the control group. That word is *much* too far out. And not very poetic, if you ask me. Old Tom prefers *'Falling of Leaves'*".

"Okay. So this leaf was part of a living structure, but at one point it became no longer useful. Imagine if leaves continued to grow on trees in winter. They would sap a lot of energy and water, giving little in return."

"And your point is …?"

"Apoptosis also applies to the human body. Ever cut yourself with a knife?"

"Although I consider myself a pretty good cook, it has happened," Tom remarked cheerfully.

"The knife will probably displace some of your skin cells from the finger surface into the finger muscle tissue," Martin said. "Now imagine if those skin cells survived and just continued to grow."

"Not sure I'd shake those hands."

"Here comes the beauty of it. Your body takes care of the problem. It sends a signal to the skin cells that they should die, go into apoptosis."

"The *falling of leaves*," Tom said and pointed his index finger at Martin. "But how does your company come into the picture?"

"Well, it happens that certain cells get out of control. The body can no longer tell them to die. Or rather, these cells have stopped listening to the signals of the body."

Martin continued his explanation even though he was starting to feel very tired. It was getting harder to find the right words.

"They have become the potential beginnings of cancer. Our aim is to develop new therapies for the treatment of cancer based on the use of apoptosis."

"Sounds pretty straightforward," Tom commented, "but a lot of companies have been doing that for many years and I haven't seen any real cancer cures yet, most people get the same old chemotherapy stuff with their hair falling out and perhaps living six more miserable months. And then the cancer just comes back again."

"Exactly. It's because cancer is not made of one single cell type. It's made of several cell types."

Tom looked puzzled.

"You confused?" Martin asked.

"Like a thirsty baby in a topless bar," Tom said with a broad grin.

Snippets of phrases started to escape Martin's attention, sleep would soon win. Instead of a smile, a yawn made its way to his face; he tried but could not hold it back.

"*Goodness gracious!* Am I that boring?!" Tom frowned.

"Sorry, it's getting late. Why don't we talk about this another day?"

Martin rubbed his eyes as they started to ache.

"No way! I want to understand now!"

Tom gave Martin a long stern look. He could be very convincing at times.

"All right, I'll try to make it short and simple," Martin said, summoning up his last resources of energy.

"Current cancer therapies aim to kill the dividing cells. But we know that a tumour has other cells, cancer stem cells. They are the 'parents' of cancer cells so to speak. They divide very rarely so you can't hit them with traditional chemotherapy.

These 'parent' cancer stem cells are most likely the reason a cancer reappears."

"I think I'm with you now." Tom was pleased with himself. "You kill those parent cancer stem cells with your drug, your *leave-falling* drug.

"That's it."

There was a short silence.

"That is really neat," Tom concluded.

"In combination with standard chemotherapy and surgery, we think we can provide the missing element and devise a real cure for cancer."

"Makes sense. You've convinced me, my friend, but I'm just a genetic idiot, so that's an easy sell." Tom finished his beer and sighed heavily.

Tom the incurable.

"Now. Over to something much more important."

Tom pulled out a hundred-franc note from his wallet and placed it carefully on the middle of the table.

"Here, Martin," he said solemnly. "Here's an up-front payment for you to go discover a molecule that makes women addicted to *just me*!"

8

'*Your husband has had an accident with his car, but he will live*' was the terse statement that the hospital gave to Menarti's wife. The twenty minutes it took her to drive to the hospital were the longest in her life. She would later find out that her husband had suffered a traumatic brain injury. The doctor called it a slight fracture of the skull with bruising.

Menarti had been at the hospital for almost two days now; he couldn't wait to get out. Already as a child he had hated hospitals. The sight and smell of blood, human suffering and antiseptics sickened him. Only God knew what kind of horrible infections he might catch from other patients during hospitalisation. At least his comprehensive health insurance had provided him with a private room.

His wife visited him each day and his children had come by. Although shocked to see the state of his body and his bruised and swollen face, they were equally surprised at the speed of his recovery. Just one day after the accident, his hospital room had been transformed into an office. With an Internet connection, a laptop, a fax machine and a landline telephone, Mr Menarti eagerly kept business rolling in this mini 'Fort Knox' he had built.

Keeping himself busy was a great remedy for pushing the pain he felt into the background and for getting through his stay in hospital, which was proving unbearable. The nurse had been quite put out when he had asked for an ultrasound scan to be postponed because of an important conference call.

Between numerous e-mails and phone calls, he thought again about how the accident had happened. His anger was always creeping back, but he managed to keep it under control. He was not going to let those young skaters go unpunished. They could have killed him. Not that they did, but it might have happened. How could he find out who they were? He had friends high up in the police force who could probably help. Some clues would be necessary.

Despite his head injury, the image of the three young men was firmly etched in his memory. Perhaps a detailed description would be enough. After all, these boys would probably hang around Lausanne in other places. The town was not huge by any means. Yes, that would be the way to go. As soon as he was out of here, he would call a few contacts he had in the police department.

With a feeling of smugness at this new resolve, he took out a pen and a pad and started to jot down every detail, no matter how small, that he could remember about the confrontation with the skaters; he even let several phone calls go unanswered.

Down the corridor, in the corner office, the head of the intensive care unit was studying the results of Menarti's abdominal ultrasound scan. On the computer screen, she could see the fine contours of the liver, the kidney and the spleen. The organs themselves seemed to be in good shape. She remembered that during the scan, the sonographer had noticed a tiny shadow on the pancreas, but the image resolution did not give a very clear picture of it. Something was not quite right and the doctor decided to follow up with a helical CT scan that would give a much better resolution in three dimensions. The only problem was that few of these machines were available in the hospital and that they were all fully booked until the following afternoon.

She thought of letting Menarti go home until then, but in the end decided to keep him in hospital. Another night or two would be safer, although, Menarti being Menarti, he would probably kick up one hell of a row.

9

In the offices of Life Technology Ventures, Kohler went to prepare another cup of espresso. The coffee machine made a deep purring sound as it crunched the beans. After dropping a small saccharine tablet into the cup, he went back into his office and sank into a comfortable black leather chair. The window behind him gave on to a partial view of the lake. The famous Geneva fountain would be turned on later in the morning and send a jet of water more than a hundred metres into the air.

The rich, bittersweet aroma of the coffee blended with the wooden scent of the furniture and the ancient parquet floor. Kohler had brought two antiques into the office to make himself feel more at home. A baroque oak cupboard and an English cabinet made out of walnut gave his office a magnificent classical look. He had often thought that this was the perfect environment for making deals on new cutting-edge technologies. The past integrating with the future.

With small careful sips of the scalding-hot coffee, he read the last quarterly report from the European Venture Capital Association. It was not very uplifting. Kohler ran his fingers through the greying strands of his sandy hair.

The past two years had been tough. He had shut down two companies that could no longer raise additional financing and several of the other companies in his portfolio were getting money at disgraceful conditions. He was often surprised to see how dreadful were the terms that the company founders, management and early investors would end up accepting.

Kohler was managing partner in a venture capital firm, Life Technology Ventures, that had 300 million Swiss francs under its control. Most of the money came from Swiss pension funds and banks. They had just raised their third fund totalling 140 million Swiss francs. This meant new investments and room for a few risky bets.

"Morning," Victor Grimau said as he appeared in the doorway to Kohler's office. He was the other partner in the firm, and he wore a bow tie at all times. According to some rumours, he had a triple-barrelled surname.

"Had a good weekend?"

"You mean Sunday evening?" Kohler twitched his mouth. "Not too bad."

"How's the chalet in Verbier coming along, is it finished yet?"

It was the usual Monday morning question.

"Getting there."

Kohler had spent most of his limited free time over the past year overseeing the construction of a specially-designed two hundred square metre luxury chalet in one of the last spots available in the centre of Verbier.

"They've started on the slate roof," he explained. "The best money can buy. I could get a two-bedroom flat for the price of that roof."

"Well, you don't really have a choice. Imagine that fine chalet with a tar-paper roof," Grimau said with a little laugh.

"You'll be right on time for the ski season." Knees bent, twisting from side to side, Grimau's style looked remarkably better indoors than on the ski slopes.

Kohler was getting tired of the subject. "So, what's cooking?"

Grimau sat down on a chair.

"Actually, I'd like to discuss the CEO in that new French company in our portfolio. What's it called now?"

"Advanced Molecular."

"Yes. Happened to drop by for their presentation at that Amsterdam biotech conference last week. You should get rid of that chap," Grimau said curtly.

"Why?"

"The man looked completely drained, there was absolutely nothing radiating from him. No energy."

"Can't really blame him, given what happened in the last financing round. But he does have many years' experience in major pharmaceuticals."

"The fellow looks like a walking charisma-bypass operation."

"Come on …" Kohler chuckled, wondering where Grimau had picked up that expression. "Why is it that we always tend to pick oversized egos as CEOs?"

"Half-psychotic bastards just seem to survive better."

Grimau seemed pleased with his statement.

Kohler walked over to his office desk to turn on his computer. "I'll tell you one thing. We're very lucky to get a guy with his experience at this early stage of the company."

"Let's hope he lasts until the next round," Grimau insisted.

"I think he will."

"I just wanted to mention it. It's your call. You're on the board of directors."

"Right. He has clear milestones for the next twelve months. If he doesn't deliver, he'll be replaced. I always back my CEOs a hundred percent – until I fire them, that is."

Kohler removed the cap from his fountain pen and placed it on the opposite end. "How are we doing on that biotech company in Lausanne … Attis Therapeutics?"

"Some of the experts have been difficult to reach because of the summer holidays," Grimau shrugged, "but the first feedback looks pretty good. Next week, we'll have the full report ready. Just one thing … aren't they at a bit too early a stage for us?"

"It's never too early for great discoveries."

"But competition in cancer is really tough. There are over four hundred new anti-cancer drugs in clinical trials. It's really crowded."

Kohler pulled out his agenda to put an end to their discussion. He glanced through the appointments of the day. "I know, Victor. But none of these drugs aim at cancer stem cells."

Back in his office, Kohler thought about the past. What a great time the late nineties had been. You couldn't help but make money. The financial markets for biotech were irrational with the hype machine running on overdrive. You bought in low and made exuberance bail you out. The more fantastic the story-line, the more money you made. Kohler had three of his companies going public on European stock exchanges in the magic year 2000. That year had made his fortune, but it had also done a lot of damage to the credibility of the industry. Many investors, public and private, had lost tons of money.

Unlike most other colleagues in the business, Kohler was now in the lucky situation of being able to retire comfortably whenever he wanted. He had promised himself that he would do so if things turned sour. It had been a close call several times these past years. The best VC days were over. Everything had become so transparent and rational. And even banks and pharma companies, for heaven's sake, were playing venture capitalists.

10

"Good morning," a calm voice greeted Martin from behind. He recognized it immediately. It was the voice of the man he had first met a year ago. A feeling of unease started to run through his body.

Broccaz had caught him by surprise. It was impossible to say where the fellow came from or how he managed to arrive so silently. The fact that he was dressed in a lab coat further added to Martin's dismay.

"Tanya made an additional lab key for me," Broccaz said, as though reading Martin's thoughts. "Sometimes I need access to the documents while the two of you are travelling."

Broccaz handled all the Attis Therapeutics accounting. Having an ex-banker manage the finances made a lot of sense. All the same, this kind of intrusion went beyond what they had agreed on.

"Why are you wearing a lab coat?" Martin asked, trying hard not to sound offensive.

"Well, I thought that I would take a peek at how my money is being spent. Nothing wrong with that, I hope?"

"No … no, of course not. It's just that I would have liked to know beforehand." Martin paused for a second. "… I could have shown you round."

"Tanya has already done that. It's interesting to see things for real."

Despite his non-scientific background, Broccaz seemed to pick up biology with incredible speed. Tanya had provided him with several university textbooks that he had begun to study eagerly. He had apparently read half of *Cell*, the bible of cell biology, in only two months. Was Broccaz doing only this and nothing else? With no wife or children to take care of, he could probably do as he pleased.

"I met some of the lab people. They seem to be working hard."

"They certainly are," Martin said, trying to gauge how much truth there was in Broccaz's unemotional voice.

"Your lab technician told me that there was a cell line infected with mycoplasma."

So that's what it was! Mycoplasma, the crabgrass of cell cultures.

"Well, apparently you were informed before me," Martin said, defensively.

"I didn't know there was a problem in the first place. You probably understand that I'd like to be kept a bit more up to date about things like that."

"We were going to tell you as soon as we had found out what it was."

Martin immediately regretted sounding naïve.

"That's okay, Mr Rieder. You've done fine so far. But, as from this week, I will set up a reporting system so that we can follow events in the lab with a little more transparency."

Martin gave Broccaz an inquisitive glance. These control measures seemed more like a declaration of distrust.

There was something unusual about Broccaz. What was it that intimidated Martin every time they met? It was not his physical appearance. Broccaz was a slightly-built man, always dressed in inconspicuous clothes. And what could be more anonymous than the lab coat he seemed so anxious to wear? His small dark-grey eyes were carefully kept behind pebble glasses and the neat, considered look on his face would melt into the wallpaper of any gathering.

Martin knew that he had seen only the tip of the iceberg, a tiny glimpse of the power and influence Broccaz had. If only half the stories Tanya told about Broccaz were true, he was a person who had the power and the connections to get anything done his way, no matter what the size of the problem. Martin was happy to have such an investor on board. It could become crucial for the success of Attis Therapeutics.

"Mr Rieder, I'm really counting on both you and Ms Karnov. We all want these therapeutic proteins to end up curing patients one fine day."

Before Martin could respond, Broccaz continued: "How much protein are you going to produce in the next batch?"

Martin thought for a moment before replying.

"We've reached very high expression levels in our E. Coli bacteria. I think they should be able to pump out enough to leave us with about ten milligrams of protein after purification."

"No more than that?" Broccaz said in a sceptical tone of voice.

"Protein-based therapeutics are more potent than the typical chemically-derived drugs. They operate with more precision, so you need much less."

"Where would that batch bring us?"

"Should be plenty for the efficacy tests we plan in new animal models."

"How about testing for toxicity?" Broccaz moved a bit closer.

"We'll do that later."

"Why not now?"

"There is just not enough protein. You need to test pretty high doses to get an idea."

"Then let's produce more. As your investor, I want to know as soon as possible if our drugs are toxic."

Martin did not entirely disagree. But then they had to produce much more protein, perhaps ten times as much. That would require a second High-Performance Liquid Chromatography machine. Those HPLC machines were not cheap.

"How much?" Broccaz asked.

"I guess somewhere around fifty thousand Swiss francs."

"Buy the machine."

"That's almost two months' worth of our current money burn rate!" Martin demurred.

The fingers of Broccaz's right hand drummed impatiently on the edge of the table.

"Well Mr Rieder, you'll just need to get things up and running with those venture capitalists."

When Broccaz left, Martin went into the office. There was a message on his answering machine from the Life Technology Ventures analyst. The voicemail had a positive note to it. They wanted to continue into further discussions.

Martin was pleased and picked up the receiver to phone him back – a first hurdle had been cleared.

The analyst needed more documents for his review. In fact, it was quite a long list. Patent information, a more detailed development plan, a more detailed twelve-month budget, a summary of the science behind therapeutic proteins and finally more information on competing academic groups. He wanted the information as soon as possible, preferably yesterday. They settled for the end of the week.

Martin hung up and let out a sigh. There was an incredible amount of work on his plate now. The piles of paper on his office desk and the floor were higher than ever.

At one point last week, he had worked for a straight thirty-six hours. Sudden hallucinations of black butterflies flying across the room had forced him to get a bit of rest. He knew it was a wake-up call from his body to announce that the limit had been reached; he tried to pull back a little. Tanya could also work long hours and would not give up until a task was accomplished. She was incredibly effective in times of stress. Despite their different personalities, he had discovered that they worked well together.

Martin checked his e-mails. In a string of uninteresting messages and spam mail were replies from two investors. He hoped for good news.

The first one read:

We regret to inform you that your company does not currently match our investment focus. However, we are interested in your scientific endeavours and would like to stay informed about the progress of your work. Please do contact us again for future financing rounds.

The second reply was a variation on the same theme. Another no-with-braces. A few lines of standard rejection in return for lengthy meetings and months of hard work.

Why did they have to pump Martin and Tanya for every piece of scientific information that had been generated over the past three years to reach this conclusion? Why didn't they just be honest and write 'thank you for a nice seminar free of charge?'

He felt disappointed and exploited. He had really thought that those investors would move forward. Suddenly all the energy and optimism from the call with the analyst from Life Technology Ventures had left him. Why did they make him do all this for nothing?

His body was aching and he did not feel the slightest enthusiasm for the two upcoming investor meetings. Would the same thing happen with a small Munich venture capital group that seemingly wanted to move forward in a hurry? And how about Dr Kohler and his colleagues from Life Technology Ventures?

As he went out into the fading sun, trying to dig up some motivation from the depths of his fatigue and his boiling anger, Martin wondered what it was all about. For the first time ever, he had the feeling that he was going round in circles and getting nowhere. What was the point of all the hard work he was putting in?

11

"**S**omeone open the windows! Quick!"
The pungent smell of inventor sweat clung tenaciously to the conference room at Life Technology Ventures after a group of four young men had left.

"Wow! We should offer people like that a bottle of deodorant as a parting gift."

Grimau pretended to be gasping for breath. His powerful eau de toilette had given up after a short battle. He walked over to the windows and opened them.

"Rejection because of bad odours?" A short chortle escaped from Kohler. "Okay, seriously. What's your take on their *win-win* proposal?"

"To get their company financed through a collaboration with one of our companies?"

"Right."

"I don't believe in win-win proposals," Grimau said resolutely. "Win-win proposals are for losers."

That blue polka-dot bow tie.

Recently, Kohler had started to hate the very sight of it. Just as the one extraordinary feature that attracts you to a person – the thing that really makes you go weak at the knees when you first notice it – over time becomes so irritating that you develop an allergy to it. Grimau's bow tie used to be original. Now it was downright ridiculous.

Kohler closed his diary and headed for the corridor.

Grimau followed him all the way to the coffee machine. "Their ultra-fast DNA sequencing technology looks interesting," he said with a keen voice. "What was the cost they mentioned of analysing the full human genome today?"

"A million Swiss francs. Still something that you and I wouldn't pay. At least not yet," Kohler said with a smile of dry amusement.

"Do you believe them? That they have a product in three years that can do it for a thousand?"

Kohler stopped and gave Grimau a sceptical glance.

"I'm not so sure. I've heard that story many times before. Everyone is aiming for the thousand-dollar human genome analysis."

Grimau impatiently rattled a key ring in his trouser pocket.

"Want one?" Kohler pushed a plastic cup under the coffee machine.

"No thanks," Grimau said pensively.

Kohler watched the cup filling up. "Don't get me wrong," he said as he dropped some saccharine in the coffee. "Their technology is very nifty. No doubt about that. But we're up against big grant money in the US. And then you have dozens of other private and public companies."

Grimau steam-rolled forward. "That would make it possible to sequence the genome of each human being in the industrialized world. Health insurance companies will be jumping up and down for joy."

Kohler sighed. "Ok, Victor. I've got too little experience with this type of business. You push it a bit further."

"What do you suggest?"

"Call our expert at Stanford and let him have a look. If their technology holds water, you trickle a bit of money into it. Five hundred thousand to reach a first validation milestone. Along with an interim CEO."

"How about Vogel?"

"You're kidding?" Kohler produced a snort of displease. "Anything with even the slightest resemblance to interpersonal skills is completely obliterated in that man. He's a bulldozer camouflaged in Armani and Rolex."

"I have a vague feeling you don't like the chap," Grimau said with a chuckle. "Anybody in mind?"

"How about Warren? You think he could get along with the founders?"

"Maybe. Anyway, we only need one of them. That guy, Eduardo, the one who sat next to you. He seemed really bright."

"And the others?" Kohler said, blowing on the hot coffee.

"The rest will just have to go. I thought of making a clean cut by founding a new company in the UK."

"No. Stay in Switzerland," Kohler said firmly. "It could backfire on our reputation. There are other ways."

In real life, Kohler had always experienced loyalty in more than two forms. It is not about being loyal or disloyal. Loyalty is deflectable. For most people, loyalty is inversely proportional to their level of desperation. At times, Kohler was surprised how easily the key company founder could be convinced that he had to get rid of his co-founders. But it was often an unpleasant experience. That sadness before the sell-out.

Outside, Martin and Tanya were sitting on comfortable white leather sofas, waiting for another meeting with Kohler and Co. Martin felt the light sweat on his back cooling down thanks to the air-conditioning. A few minutes later, he and Tanya were led into the meeting room where the woman analyst was waiting for them with a fresh notepad. Kohler entered with Grimau, greeted his guests and went straight to the point.

"Great to see both of you again. I think we are making some good progress here, but I'm afraid we just have half an hour for our discussion today. Grimau and I have to leave for other meetings."

There was something unusual about Kohler. Several of the other VCs Martin had met behaved like gods with an accompanying aura of arrogance. Perhaps it was the inevitable long-term outcome of being surrounded by too many knee-crawling entrepreneurs. Kohler seemed detached from the superiority syndrome.

Tanya did well in presenting the recent lab data, but chronic fatigue was also starting to take its toll on her. The ensuing questions were tough, but they were all relevant and showed clearly that the analyst had done her homework. One of the main issues was the specificity and potential side effects of their drugs. Could the drug have an effect on healthy cells? The side effects could be disastrous if you killed bone marrow cells as well. They discussed at length which lab tests were deemed necessary to clarify this aspect.

Towards the end of the meeting, Grimau commented on the name, an impossible six-letter acronym, of their drug.

"You have to get rid of that cryptic designation. When drugs go into pre-clinical and clinical development, you always give them a simple code name that somehow links them to your company."

"Such as?"

"Some letters from your company name and then a number."

"Like A-1?"

"Sounds more like a new aircraft." Grimau scratched his head. "People may think that you just went ahead with the first molecule you found."

"Which is almost what happened. We modified the first molecule we found," Tanya intervened.

"That doesn't give a very professional impression."

"I don't understand," Tanya said.

"Despite what people think, the pharmaceutical industry is terribly old-fashioned and very unsophisticated in coming up with new drugs. Most of them work with a huge robotized high-throughput research machinery. Like an automated lotteryticket choosing system, where they hope that testing millions of molecules at high speed will help them fish out the winning molecule more quickly. That's why they spend over a billion Swiss francs for every new drug that comes on the market. In biotech we can be much more creative and smarter. And we avoid the big overhead costs and the fancy hotels."

"What does that have to do with us?" Tanya questioned.

"Former executives of these pharma companies are sitting everywhere, including in many venture capital companies. Many of them like grey hair and things done the old way," Grimau said.

Kohler looked at his watch. Window-dressing was not his field of interest. Before he could speak, Grimau continued. "How about coding your drug something like ATS-187? ATS for Attis Therapeutics and then some three- or four-digit number. Any number."

"But drugs normally have real names. Like Aspirin or Zolpidem," Martin commented.

"Hope you don't need too much of them," Kohler said with an inquiring smile. "In general, drugs get names instead of codes when chances are high that they will reach the market. At that stage, some major pharma or biotech company will most likely have obtained a licence from you and will take care of the final clinical trials and marketing the drug."

Tanya and Martin nodded in silence.

"You are aware, aren't you, that both of you lack business and drug development experience?" Grimau asked.

"We've been told that before, but isn't it the case for most other start-ups?" Martin replied.

"Would it be a problem for you if we found people with that experience?"

"All we want is to work with people we can trust," Martin said.

"Good, that comes pretty close to our objectives."

Time was up; Grimau and Kohler had to leave in a rush for their meetings and promised to get back within a week. Despite the rather short length of the meeting, both Tanya and Martin were pleased with the session. All the questions pointed to a significant degree of interest, indicating that they were not far from the next step: term sheet discussions for a financing round.

Martin felt great after the meeting. The chemistry definitely worked and they were getting closer to a deal. The steps were small, granted, but they were getting there.

And Kohler's handshake had been unusually long.

12

Menarti eventually had his CT scan done and was keen to leave the clinic. The whole situation was getting close to plain torture. He sensed that they were not telling him everything they knew when they made him drink that horrible barium sulphate contrast dye: this would show up as fluorescent colours on the scanner.

It was the worst thing he had ever come across, and it smelled like grapes going rotten. The awful chalky aftertaste had hung on in his throat the whole day long. In reaction to this, he threw an increasing number of insults at the nurses and doctors who dared to interrupt him as he worked busily from his hospital bed.

Results of the CT scan came back in next to no time – just as well, for both Menarti and the hospital staff.

The head of the intensive care unit sat quietly in the corner room at the end of the corridor. She was thinking about how she could tell Menarti the very mixed news she was looking at. The good part was that the accident would not have any deleterious consequences.

The bad news, unfortunately, would overshadow everything else. Despite Menarti's abrasiveness, she felt sorry for him. No human being deserved to have the condition they had discovered by pure coincidence.

Pancreatic cancer, one of the most deadly cancers, with no available cure. The scanning images showed that the cancer had started spreading to the stomach and the lymph nodes. Tissue samples taken with a needle aspiration biopsy had confirmed the diagnosis.

Menarti's first reaction to the news was a surprise to her. He simply didn't believe the results. In a state of rage, he called her an *incompetent idiot* and demanded a transfer to a hospital with *real* medical doctors where the scanning and the analyses could be performed correctly. The oncology department head was called in and Menarti eventually had to accept the dreadful news.

He had felt pain in his abdomen before the accident, but had never paid any attention to it. The pain had always been worse after eating, so he had started to eat less and had lost ten kilos in six months, much to his pride. It was of little comfort that he could thank those young roller-skating fools who had almost killed him for helping him find out that he had an illness that would indeed take his life.

In his hospital bed, he tried hard to stay calm and think logically, wondering why God had allowed this to happen. So this was life's return for all he had given?

Despair was closer than ever as he tried to come to terms with the reality. Today's treatment protocols could increase to about one in five his chances of living another year.

To hell with these statistics! They were just numbers from doctors and scientists to drive you mad.

Sure, modern medicine could do wonders – just not for him.

Menarti turned to the side and took out a disc from the drawer next to the bed. He inserted it into a CD player, pushed the repeat button and put on the earphones.

I'll fight.

He held up the cover of his favourite composer. A disfigured hooked nose, dark grey eyes radiating with benevolence. The famous man's features had an unusual combination of the attractive and the repulsive. Like many in his day, Haydn was a survivor of smallpox, his face pitted with the scars of the disease.

13

The scorching late summer heat continued to break new temperature records across Switzerland; not a single drop of rain had fallen for what seemed like an eternity. With the money set aside for the new HPLC machine, severe drought had also hit the Attis Therapeutics bank account, now holding just enough money for another three months. Martin had tightened all the bolts on lab expenses to the absolute maximum.

Four different investors, including one from Germany, had shown interest in Attis, but none had yet taken the plunge. They were definitely eager about it, with a seemingly endless desire for more information.

Before this experience, Martin had always believed that venture capitalists were dynamic go-getters. This seemed more like some kind of waiting game. But what were they all waiting for? For risk to go away?

The upholstery of the armchair Martin was sitting in had seen better days. He tried to read a biotech business article, but his thoughts escaped again and again. To the exciting moment one year ago, at the huge leather-covered desk in the notary's office when they signed the legal documents and Attis Therapeutics had become reality. The first results and patents and the dreams about becoming the next Genentech.

And the fight with old professor Larousse who used his position at the University to get a stake in the company, eyeing a chance to get a last kick out of his uneventful life. But even that problem, for some reason, had solved itself with relative ease. Larousse abruptly retired three years ahead of time, sold his home and moved to a summerhouse in Provence with his wife. Martin was surprised by the swiftness of all these events and suspected that Broccaz somehow had had a finger in the pie.

He stared out of the lab-office window.

Where had all the fun gone?

He had spent two great years at the University of South California, where he did his post-doctoral research on crystallizing new proteins. Although he was somewhat prejudiced against Los Angeles – Tom always said that if you got up early enough in LA, you could hear the birds coughing in the trees – Martin soon discovered the enjoyable diversity of the people there. His initial scorn for loud-mouthed, self-absorbed American culture in relentless one-dimensional pursuit of money soon turned into admiration for its youthfulness and optimism.

The move back home from California had been difficult. Everything suddenly seemed small. From the small cars squeezing into narrow streets to the packages of undersized frozen spring rolls you had to stuff into a cramped freezer compartment in a tiny fridge that still seemed too big for the pocket-sized kitchens. Compared to the United States, life here suddenly seemed constrained and limited, asphyxiated by a tightness that covered everything. Martin had not once had an attack of claustrophobia all the time he was in the USA. Only months after returning, it started to come back again.

Was his return to Switzerland just the same experience as the mistaken sensation of speed you have after leaving a motorway, when everything seems unbelievably slow for the first few moments until your mind gently recalibrates itself to the new pace?

The quality of life in Switzerland was, after all, superb. People would go to great lengths to stay in this zone of terrific comfort. The scenery, the security, the stability – all increasingly scarce resources elsewhere in the world.

Martin threw the article on the table, rubbed his face, and looked all round the office. As usual it was full of untidy heaps of notes, journals, annuals and student periodicals. Above the door of the lab office, on a narrow ledge, dust was gathering on two empty bottles of champagne.

It had been so exciting in those early days setting up the lab with all the bartering that had had to be done for second-hand equipment. The intensive sessions with government-sponsored coaches and experts. And all the many accomplishments and late Friday afternoons with worry-free beers. Every week brought new and unexpected events, not always best news, but things seemed to keep moving forward.

No, he would not give up. There were ups and downs in every start-up, it was all just part of the game. The good times would come back again. They always did at some point.

Martin stood up and decided to pay a visit to the labs. If the investors did not budge, Attis would have to.

Deep in concentration, Tanya was standing over a phase contrast microscope with the different samples of tissue cultures. They were taken from the back of the mice on which grafted cells from human pancreatic cancer tissue had been growing.

Tanya moved only to exchange samples, momentarily taking her eyes off the magnified images of blue dots scattered over an ocean of pink-purple shades. Carefully, she inserted the next sample and stared into the micro-universe again.

The blue spots were the nuclei of the cells and proof that the cells had been alive and growing when the staining was performed. The strong purple colours came mainly from blood vessel staining; the cancer cells had developed their own improved blood supply system to facilitate their uncontrolled growth.

A few green cells, barely visible in the sample, were the most interesting detail. The green spots came from the staining of the cancer stem cells. Tanya had used a completely new dye and coupled it to an antibody that would seek out a specific target in the stem cell cancer membrane. Thanks to her improvements, the dye would make it much easier to detect individual cells.

"Martin, come and have a look."

Tanya stepped back from the microscope and waved him over.

"Not bad, but there are still some cancer cells left," Martin said, slightly disappointed, keeping both eyes on the lenses of the microscope. He had hoped that the whole tumour would have been wiped clean.

"True enough. But what has disappeared?" Tanya said with a triumphant tone.

"Let me see," Martin turned a button on the side to sharpen the picture.

"Green … there are no green spots!" Martin looked up.

"No more pancreatic cancer stem cells!" Tanya said with a big smile.

They looked at the other samples as well. Not a single green dot could be found.

"Tanya. I'll be damned … that's just fantastic!"

Martin could not hold back the sparks of excitement flaring up within him. He gave Tanya a firm hug.

"Wow! That is an amazing result. You know what this means? This will make the investors move."

Finally some good news. Finally the lifeline they had hungered so much for. Now the fruits of all their hard work were truly appearing.

74

Martin wanted, no, he *needed* to celebrate.

"Get the lab people together. I'm back in ten minutes with some stuff."

Bubbling with excitement, he ran over to the local supermarket, filled up two boxes with crisps and bottles of champagne and made several joking remarks as he paid the cashier. This could be big, this could be the start of a new paradigm in cancer treatment. To Martin, these new results were irrefutable; the VCs would have a hard time arguing against them. What if the roles now finally were to be reversed? The VCs would be running after their company in a bidding game that Martin would find so sweet.

Still in a daydream, he returned to the lab office and cleared the paper that was scattered over the large office table. As the corks started to pop and the late afternoon unfolded with laughter and joy, Martin felt that the tide was about to turn. The torment had not been in vain and the sun of pay-day was finally starting to rise in all of its splendour above the horizon.

14

The investors reacted differently to the amazing news from the lab.

They were not jumping up and down in sheer joy as Martin had hoped. The results did seem to impress them, but they were still not taking any initiatives about moving forward.

In everything he had undertaken in the past, Martin had been able to influence the course of events in one way or another. This time, however, he felt completely helpless. The more he tried, the more stuck the situation seemed to become. During the past weeks, he had relentlessly pushed on all fronts: investors, technicians, Tanya. The only thing moving was the money that was still trickling out of the Attis bank account.

Martin was beginning to have serious misgivings about it all. Attis Therapeutics' financial situation now suddenly appeared terribly fragile. He thought of the scenario where they would run out of money with no other option but to fire all the lab technicians and shut down the company. A scenario in which he would lose all the money he had borrowed from his uncle to start the company, his father having fiercely opposed any such risky madness.

One person would probably be happy, though. Professor Larousse would get his sweet revenge for having been excluded from the start-up and probably sit laughing on his sun-sheltered Provence veranda, a glass of iced *pastis* in his hand.

If only you had listened to me.

If only he had been born into a rich family like Gavin's son Lorne, that lucky fellow, things would have been so much easier. All this would not be happening.

What about Sarah? If he ultimately had to decide between her and Attis, he knew what choice he would make. But why did he have to choose? It wasn't fair. Attis' struggle was his struggle. Why did he have to suffer in this way to be successful? Apparently, there were no easy ways, no simple shortcuts.

Despite all the bother, Martin remained confident that Sarah understood the importance of what he was up to. But the gap between her mental and emotional understanding could sometimes be dangerously wide.

The phrase *'Of course, take your time'* can have many meanings when said by a woman. And said by Sarah it could mean just about anything. Body language and voice tonality would provide the next clue. The bandwidth would go from *'No problem, go and relax over a beer with Tom'* to *'We never go out together'* to *'If you're not here in five minutes, I'll personally kick your backside'*.

Lately, Martin had needed no body language skills to understand that Sarah was closer to the hard-hitting end of the scale.

The word 'neglect' could be heard loudly several times during the heated discussions, that Spanish blood of hers reaching boiling point more often than ever before. At first, he tried to argue with her. But he knew very well that at certain times it would be best to simply shut up.

Just another three months, Sarah. Please. Then I'm done.

One evening after a fierce cat-and-dog fight, he ended standing behind Sarah with his arms folded around her and the chair she was sitting on. He kissed the beautiful copper skin of her neck, slowly breathing in the natural scent of her long jet-black hair. He suddenly recalled how it smelled, naturally, like finely-roasted hazel nuts. Even blindfolded, he was certain he could recognize her fragrance from that of any other woman.

Then he said that he was sorry. They remained silent for a little while and both felt the sharp energy from the released frustrations slowly turning into a trickling desire for each other. Sarah turned towards him, her deep eyes searching his face.

She stood up, holding her lips just next to his ears, whispering.

"Please … don't destroy yourself," she said. "It's not worth it."

"I won't. I promise."

She looked sceptically at him.

"I wish you would listen."

In one quick movement, she bit him in the lower lip and they met in a fierce kiss. Martin's hands held her firmly. Then he pushed her hard on to the bed. As they moved their bodies together, against each other, with each other, it seemed as though all their torments had disappeared for a while, for a moment beyond time. They were somewhere in space, untouchable, oscillating with a new and unfamiliar intensity.

Later that night Martin woke up thirsty and tired. All the thoughts flowing back into his mind prevented him from falling asleep again. He drank several glasses of milk and went back to bed, watching Sarah sleep peacefully. After tossing and turning for a while, he got up and went out on to the living-room balcony to look at the half-moon outside. It seemed to stare at him with a knowing glint. He remembered when, as a young boy, he believed the moon was following him. Whenever he moved, the moon seemed to follow in the same direction. No matter how fast he moved. It was his friend and a nice illusion. Until he learned the truth. The uncomfortable adult matter-of-fact truth.

Now the moon was poking reality right into his face again. He had tried to sleep but in vain. It was unfair. His entire body craved for sleep. One thought followed the other with increasing speed and density through his brain like rush-hour tube trains. All the problems of the past day started on auto-replay. It was as if, after a temporary respite, all the stress came striding back with steps that became firmer with every new thought entering his mind.

15

Saturday evening finally arrived as a little oasis of relief from an arduous week. Martin stood beside Sarah in the street next to her car. They were getting ready to leave for dinner with the Falcrofts.

"I can't believe it – what on earth is that?" He grimaced in disgust.

"A car!" Sarah replied, shrugging her dark tanned shoulders over her cornflower-blue tube-shaped top. She had spent a lot of time deciding what to wear on this hot late-September evening.

"Okay. But that definition doesn't include a four-wheeled rubbish-bin."

Martin cocked his head to one side. Sarah looked stunning, but it was not enough to prevent him feeling irritated. "When we bought it a year ago, it still resembled a Golf GTI. Some years old, perhaps, but … still a car."

"For God's sake Martin, it's just a machine."

"Right now, I'd say it doesn't even look like that. More like one big stain. Oops, hang on …" Martin let his fingers run over the surface of the car and said ironically, "I think there's some metal underneath after all!"

"Come on! A good shower of rain will take it all off."

"Yes, but the rain won't take care of the inside – no matter how hard it falls." Martin opened the door. "Look at this! I can't believe it! Half of a *baguette* from … let's guess, yesterday."

"Relax Martin."

"You always criticize the way I forget things in the fridge. Why should a car be allowed to develop its own biotope if a fridge can't?"

Sarah glared at him.

"It's *my* car!" she exploded. "You continue like that and I'll go alone! Don't be such a bloody nitpicker."

Martin sighed. "All I'm asking for is a tiny bit of respect for what we own. We're not exactly filthy rich."

"Okay, point taken. Over and out. Now, how about if we just travelled in your car to the Falcrofts?"

"I think we should."

Twenty minutes later, they were walking up the stairs to the Falcroft family home. Martin pushed the button on the door frame and a sound like church bells echoed from somewhere deep inside. After a few moments, Lindsey opened the door. Popper and Finch came flying out past them to inspect the tyres of the unfamiliar object in the courtyard.

Lindsey welcomed them in the traditional Swiss-French style with a *bise*. Instead of the typical airy kisses, she planted three successive smackers on their cheeks with a firm hug. The wild yellow colour of her dress radiated like the sun.

She led them into the house, which was kept cool by its thick stone walls. It was a sumptuous home, but still modest in size compared to the vast garden. This seemed to be a house built with a different philosophy from most other houses. It was not built to entertain its residents. It did not have large surfaces of glass that would provide a beautiful view of a picturesque garden and the lake.

Gavin and Lindsey's dwelling had a different purpose. It was a place for timelessness. A shelter for people returning home, exhausted by excessive exposure to the world – the daily stress, the faltering economies, the traffic jams, the raging wars. It had a remarkable atmosphere of tranquillity and peace.

"Let's go and find my two menfolk," Lindsey said.

The herringbone parquet floor creaked as they walked across the lounge. Logs were stacked inside a vast fireplace, ready for the first signs of colder days to come. Martin imagined the fire lit in wintertime, sending a warm glow over the massive oak table that stood in front of it.

Gavin rose slowly from a dark brown leather chair to greet them.

"Hello my dear young friends. I am so glad to see both of you." He held a glass of milky liquid in one hand, with a halfsmoked cigar between his fingers. Martin looked at Sarah, an antismoking fanatic under normal circumstances, but she held back for some reason; the cigar had, as it were, its rightful place in this house, its smoke blending softly into the décor.

"How about a little glass of absinthe, the artists' elixir?"

Martin loved the way Gavin pronounced the word 'artist' with a strong Scottish burr of the 'r'. His words seemed to come from somewhere deep in his throat rather than from his mouth.

"I'm not sure Sarah's fine palate is made for absinthe," Lindsey said. "That's a man's drink. Would you like a glass of white wine instead, my dear?"

Sarah was more than happy to have some wine.

"I can see on his face that Martin wants one," Gavin said, "I'll prepare it."

He poured a handsome amount of the strong transparent liquid into a glass, placed a flat strainer across it and dropped a lump of sugar on the strainer. Then he picked up a pitcher and slowly let some drops of water fall on to the sugar cube. After a short while, the edges of the cube began to dissolve. He poured some more water over the cube and finally used the strainer to give the drink a quick stir. The liquid had turned milky green. *La fée verte.* The green fairy.

"Let's have a toast to the myth that came with keeping absinthe clandestine and to the country that invented it," Gavin said, holding up his glass.

Martin had never tried absinthe before. The liquid curled its way through his throat. A bit like *pastis*, but then again very different. Many more nuances, not just liquorice.

"Don't drink too much of it. It contains toxins that will shortcircuit your brain," Lindsey said.

Protesting strongly, Gavin embarked on a long lecture about absinthe. How it was made from wormwood and how it had been used in the old days to treat everything from stomach infections to liver and gall bladder problems.

"Medicine, *mon œil!*" Lindsey said disapprovingly, pulling one eyelid down over her eye with her index finger. "Artists have gone nuts and killed themselves because of it."

Gavin smacked his lips. "You don't have to end up slicing off your earlobe if you just drink a glass once in a while with some friends. And the absinthe you can buy in the shops today contains almost no thujone."

"Interesting choice," Lorne said from the doorway.

Gavin took a large sip from his glass.

"Lorne has chosen a third option," he scoffed. "Complete abstinence. He'll be drinking water the whole evening. Pity, because I'm going to fetch some pretty decent wines."

Lorne walked over and greeted Sarah and Martin. He told Sarah that he loved the feng shui touch in her garden plans. He was about to make a couple of further suggestions when Lindsey broke in.

"There is one important thing still missing. Could you come up with an idea as to how we can get some shade on the terrace? It gets so hot these days with the sun shining directly on it. I don't fancy venetian blinds."

Sarah had several ideas. In the midst of an excited discussion as to what plants could offer the best shade, Gavin saw an opportunity to grab Martin to help him choose some good wine. They went downstairs to the basement. Gavin had built a wine cellar inside the mandatory anti-atomic shelter that most people now used as food storage rooms since the end of the Cold War.

As he slowly pulled open the two-ton steel-reinforced concrete door, a large selection of wines came into sight. A humidifier and an air conditioner stood at the other end of the room.

"Not the worst place to spend time during a nuclear attack," Martin said jokingly. Then he noticed the only food available, a large stack of cans of tuna fish on the floor and added "… at least the first night."

Gavin gave a short burst of hearty laughter then took out some dusty bottles of wine.

"From the little I know of you, I can tell that you're not much of a liar, son. Not that I think you should be. I like honest people. But when you do business, try not to give too much away."

"The poker-face approach?" Martin said. "Don't know if that would help with venture capitalists anyway."

"Martin, if you need some help with your company, you can always call on me. I'm not a biotech expert but I've some experience that could be useful."

"Is there any general advice you could give me?"

Gavin looked through the stacks of bottles, humming cheerfully.

"I wish I could give you the recipe for success," he said, "but I'm not sure one exists. It's a moving target. The world changes, you see." He turned round. "But I can give you a great recipe for failure: trying to please everybody at the same time."

Now he had it, the perfect lead-in to the question Martin had been bursting to ask ever since they had first met. As things stood with the start-up right now, he badly needed Gavin by his side.

"Would you be interested in joining the Attis board of directors?"

Gavin seemed unprepared for the question and made an unusual split-second stutter. "Very flattering ... but ... you know, I would really prefer to advise you personally. Sometimes it's better not to mix business and friendship."

When they came back with bottles of carefully selected red and white wines, Martin noticed that Sarah was in deep conversation with Lorne at the dinner table while Lindsey was preparing food in the kitchen. He heard Lorne talking to her about Chinese medicine and the advantages of a holistic approach over the specialized kind of medicine practised in the West.

"Shouldn't you be offering to help Lindsey?" Martin said abruptly with a note of irritation in his voice.

"I did – and she refused," Sarah replied somewhat resentfully.

He would have loved to participate and challenge Lorne, but held back. Everything about the fellow irritated him. Lorne was the exact opposite of all that Martin believed in: the archetype of a spoiled, lazy, rich man's child, pampered his whole life long, his slightest whims satisfied. He wondered how Gavin could have allowed that to happen.

Adding to Martin's annoyance was the fact that he hadn't seen Sarah looking so enthusiastic for as long as he could remember. He observed her as she ran her fingers through the thickness of her long black hair. She really looked gorgeous tonight.

No bloody need for lessons in body language, Martin thought as he swallowed the remaining absinthe in one gulp. He wondered if she did this on purpose to play on his jealousy. *We'll talk about this later.*

Gavin opened the bottle of white *Meursault* and decanted it into a carafe through a funnel, using a coffee filter.

"This wine's almost as old as you people," Gavin said. "Quite a lot of deposit already." He held up the filter and pointed at some grey residue in the bottom of it. "Some have more deposit than others. Just like humans," he joked. "Not necessarily a bad sign."

Gavin sampled the wine.

"Perfect! What a taste! Almost like sherry. Look at that golden colour!" He took another euphoric sip. "This wine is just like me. We've both reached a point where we can start bragging about our age."

Lindsey served the first course, a delicious *saumon en croûte* with loads of melted butter. She had cooked enough food to serve an entire village. The discussion during the meal covered many of Gavin's favourite topics and he made certain that Martin's glass was never less than half-full.

"What I prefer is the men's 100-metres," Gavin said as they were talking about the recent Olympic games.

Lindsey frowned. "I think we should boycott the whole thing. All the athletes are doped. It's not like it used to be."

"They are not," Gavin said.

"Of course they are," Lindsey insisted.

"No they're not! Not all of them. There is one sport where the players are never doped up," Gavin said with a knowing smile. He helped himself to several more spoonfuls of salmon. "Curling. I don't think you'll find any curling players on drugs."

Martin laughed. "Okay, but the people who invented that sport must have been on something! Maybe a drunken farmer losing a big Emmental cheese on an icy road. Seeing it sliding down the street."

Lorne too was smiling.

"And the Olympic committee that accepted that as a sport?

They probably had too much wine as well that day!" Martin went on, tears of laughter running down his cheeks.

Gavin, suddenly serious, got to his feet.

"Curling was invented by the Scots!" he almost bellowed, "It was one of the biggest national games in the whole of Scotland in the eighteenth century."

Sarah looked contemptuously at Martin. She had that special expression on her face that always seemed to be there whenever he had gone beyond a certain level of alcohol consumption.

There was a brief silence.

"But, you're right … it's still a pretty daft kind of game!" Gavin's laugh came bursting out in a tremendous roar.

He raised his glass.

"Here's to curling and the poker-face approach!"

The main course was a haunch of red deer with walnuts and *spätzli*. Gavin, who did most of the talking during the meal, said that he had insisted on something substantial for the evening. Since he had developed a strong aversion to the 'fluffy vegetable salad stuff' during summer, he wanted to jump-start the venison season. Nothing less than an *Amarone* from the 'insanely great year of 1997' would do for such a meal.

"How do you feel about your start-up experience?" Lorne asked at a moment when Gavin was chewing eagerly on a piece of meat.

"*Feel* about it?" Martin repeated. He had not anticipated that kind of question. What he was really feeling right now was the rather intoxicating result of Gavin's generosity with the wine during dinner.

"Well … hum … I hope it's more than just a *feeling experience*. This is for real, it's not a game."

Martin went on to explain as best as he could the breakthrough discoveries they had made in the lab, the potential for cancer cure, his struggle with venture capitalists.

"The stress is real enough. Gives him plenty of sleep problems," Sarah commented.

"Oh!" Lindsey said. "Aren't you a bit young for that?"

"Many successful people don't sleep much," Martin retorted. "I'll sleep when I get old."

"Don't bet on that!" Gavin picked the last bits of meat from a bone. "Perhaps you should think of getting a business person on board now."

"You mean an MBA type of person?"

"Let me tell you something about MBAs," Gavin said, scowling.

"Here he goes again." Lindsey rolled her eyes.

"I once interviewed this chap, fresh out of business school. A good school, mind you. He'd worked three years before taking his MBA and I asked him what position he was aiming for. He said marketing director would be fine but what he was really going for was a Vice Presidency – my company was quite small at the time. I told him that I could offer him a salary of a hundred and forty thousand pounds, plus an entire benefit package including a high-end BMW."

Gavin poured another round of wine for himself and Martin.

"Then this MBA bloke starts to look a bit nervous and says 'I can't believe it, you must be kidding' and then I go 'Aye – but you started it all!'"

Gavin burst into a howl of laughter.

Martin couldn't help laughing too.

"You're so rude." Lindsey shook her head, almost in contempt.

"A wee bit o' fun is hard to come by these days. And in this country you have to invent it all by yourself. Try watching Swiss television. Ever see anything funny there? Thank God for the BBC and satellite dishes."

"There's this Swiss guy dressed up as a woman. What's his name again?" Lindsey said.

"Marie-Thérèse Porchet," Sarah said.

"Porsche?" Gavin looked surprised.

Martin broke out into an exaggerated giggle.

"Porchet. Pronounced the same way. But she ..., he, is very entertaining; performs mostly in Paris."

"That doesn't mean he's funny," Gavin objected. "Deviousness and joking are not the same thing. The French have never really understood the difference."

"They probably think you're sarcastic and rude," Lindsey said, just to keep Gavin on his mettle.

"Well, I prefer old-fashioned humour, people being their spontaneous selves. Now why is that so difficult?" Gavin commented.

"Most people find it rather difficult," Lorne said.

"Oh ... so we're getting to the philosophical part of the evening." Gavin decided it was the perfect moment to go to the toilet.

In his absence, silence fell as though a plug had been pulled out of the conversation. Lindsey excused herself and went out to prepare the sweet course in the kitchen.

Lorne, rubbing his chin thoughtfully with his thumb and index finger, looked at Martin. "Can I ask you another question?"

"Fine. On you go ... If it's not too tricky. Your dad's wine is beginning to ... well, marinate my brains."

Sarah gave Martin another cold look.

"Are you prepared to go all the way?" Lorne asked.

"I've been going all the way for some time now," Martin said cheerfully. "You have to go through some pain if you want to reach Nirvana. When I was a boy, my father said something I've never forgotten: 'Nothing comes of its own volition – except dirty nails'." Martin chuckled childishly and took another large sip of wine. He was starting to feel dizzy, but he was so irritated by Lorne's presence that he remained alert.

"One of the forgotten rules of the universe," Lorne laughed.

Martin could no longer tell if this was meant in good part or if Lorne was actually making fun of him. Sarah laughed for the first time that evening.

"My turn," Martin said in a somewhat provocative tone. "I have a question for you, my friend: what do *you* believe in?"

"I believe that all things have a *telos*." Lorne said. "The Greek word for *end* or *purpose*. Living life with a purpose. Aristotle had the idea that all things have a 'telos', a noble end or goal to which they must give expression."

The falling of leaves, Martin thought. He could not get rid of that annoying phrase since the evening on the balcony with Tom.

"A seed's highest telos is to grow into a plant," Lorne continued, "the lyre player's is to become an accomplished harpist. In anything you do you have the choice of doing it using your highest self and your best talents."

So what about leaves? Did leaves also have a telos? Or were they just serving the telos of the tree?

Martin wanted to ask Lorne what his aim in life was, but he was interrupted by Gavin coming back in with a box of cigars and a bottle of cognac.

"Martin's *telos* is to grow into a good CEO."

An expression of delight came over Martin's face. Gavin continued: "Chief Exaggeration Officer … that title impresses young women."

"Gaaavin!" Lindsey shouted through the serving hatch.

"Mr CEO. Would you like a cigar?"

"I wouldn't actually …"

"Mr CEO, in your position, it would be absolutely incorrect to refuse a cigar. We'll smoke it in the library. You have the choice between an Epicure and a Magnum 46. Which do you prefer?"

Martin looked at Sarah. She stared him straight in the eye for several seconds. He looked away and turned towards Gavin.

"Epicure sounds okay by me."

16

That dinner with the Falcrofts ended in another heated quarrel between Sarah and Martin. Shortly after Gavin and Martin had gone out for a walk to finish smoking their cigars, the sound of engines and loud yelling could be heard in front of the house. A curious sight awaited the rest of the party: two cars driving around in circles in the courtyard, Martin in Gavin's Jaguar and Gavin in Martin's Clio.

Sarah did not begrudge Martin having a bit of fun – relieving all the hard work and stress. Surprised by Gavin's behaviour, though, she was struck by the possibility that the brains of some elderly British men may indeed be wired slightly differently from those of other people. She found it hard to imagine him ever being playful like that with Lorne, the lone wolf, living inside the thoughts and ideas he had picked up from all corners of the world. Sarah had the impression that Lorne was trying to make sense of it all, seeking the common denominators that held everything together. She could have listened to his unusual and fascinating lines of thought forever. She wished that Martin would just for once take the time to do the same.

The trouble had started when Martin came back into the living room and saw Lorne with his hand placed over hers. She regretted having instinctively withdrawn her hand as soon as she caught sight of Martin, making him jump to all the wrong conclusions. Her explanation on the way back home about Lorne reading her aura had only added fuel to the fire. Martin had been furiously angry with her. Never in their three-year relationship had she seen him jealous like that. But Sarah was unwilling to accept any accusations and the stage was set for another tooth-and-nail fight that took most of the following day to fade away.

For Martin, the weekend was supposed to be a time of rest, a deep breath of oxygen, but it was now anything but that. The fight with Sarah had scared him. For the first time since they had met, the possibility of their relationship breaking up seemed suddenly terribly real to him. He was not sure if his nerves could stand another round of fierce bickering with her. Why was it that both his professional and private life seemed to have connived to make everything so miserable for him?

A heavy storm, together with a loose shutter from some neighbouring flat or other kept him awake for most of Sunday night; early on Monday morning, Martin thought he would never be able to get up to go to work. His entire body was aching and he felt more exhausted than ever. Were there no limits to what he had to endure? He could not go on like this for much longer. Something had to give.

The only small, indeed tiny, light at the end of the tunnel that kept his head just above water was a somewhat cryptic message left on the lab answering machine from the German venture capital firm in Munich, Upfront Ventures. He had listened to it several times from home to be sure he had deciphered it correctly. Norbert Regenhofer, the managing partner of Upfront Ventures, was now ready to take things 'another step forward', whatever that meant.

Full of strong coffee, Martin dragged himself to the lab and, as usual, was the first one in. He unlocked the door and went into his office. He opened the adjoining walk-in cupboard to find his stained mug where he had left it two days before, standing next to the tiny sink, which was mostly used to clean the few pieces of cutlery they all shared.

As he poured water into the electric kettle, Martin suddenly found himself on the alert. Something's not right, he thought. Not right at all.

He could not pinpoint what it was. Things just did not fit. He walked into the lab, which was in a pretty awful shape again. The whole place was impregnated with sloppiness.

Tanya, for God's sake, he thought angrily. *All this mess is killing me.*

But the mess was different today. Instead of the innocent random disorder from inexperienced enthusiasm, there was something troubling him about the lab. He stepped back against the wall and started to take a mental picture of all the items in the room. What was it exactly that disturbed him so much?

He tried to compare what he could see with the pictures in his memory. Were the instruments in their usual place? He checked them all twice just to make sure. Even the new HPLC machine stood exactly where he had left it for the weekend. So, logically speaking, everything was all right. Yet he new it wasn't.

That strange feeling.

Like when you sense that somebody is watching you. A stare that touches the back of your neck with infinite lightness, yet you know that it's there – and you turn around to meet the other person's eyes.

But there were no other eyes, and still he felt that he was being stared at. A scrutinizing glare that coldly observed every little detail. Then a far-fetched idea struck him: could someone be spying on them with a hidden camera or a bugging device? Professor Larousse who had retired so suddenly? Or maybe Broccaz?

Martin found a screwdriver and, frantically, started to dismantle one instrument after the other. After fifteen minutes of fruitless searching, he felt droplets of perspiration all over his forehead.

He stood back for a moment. This was absolutely ridiculous. Was this all a trick that his nerve-wracked mind was playing on him? He was glad nobody was around to see him like this. They'd think he'd gone crazy.

Just as he was about to re-assemble the last of the lab computers, the main door opened. Listening to the light, quick footsteps, Martin could tell it was Tanya. He closed his eyes and took a deep breath to focus himself. Perhaps he shouldn't say anything to her about this. Hopefully she would notice herself. He went out to greet her.

"Morning Martin. You okay? You look very ... exhausted," she said.

"Thanks. Just what a tired person needs to hear." Martin said with irony and cleared his throat. This morning's bleary-eyed stare that came back from the mirror had told him exactly the same thing, but right now this was the least of his worries.

He made an effort to speak calmly, as if nothing unusual had happened. "I was just in the lab. It's a total mess there, Tanya. Let me show you."

Tanya took off her jacket and slipped into a lab coat without saying anything. On the way to the lab, he hoped she would catch that worrying sensation as well.

He watched her carefully as they stood in the doorway.

"You notice anything different?" he asked as they stood in the doorway.

"We'll get that cleared up quickly," she replied.

"Nothing unusual?" he ventured carefully.

"No." Tanya paused. "Martin, are you okay?"

"Something isn't right." He almost whispered. "I think we are being observed, but I can't explain it."

"Martin, we're both very stressed-out right now. The best thing is to try to relax."

He was angered by what he judged to be a condescending tone.

"Relax? We've got three months of money left. Three months! Then it's over, Tanya."

"Come on. If we don't make it, there will be other things."

"Perhaps for you. Attis or no Attis. Your career is on track. Not for me. I don't want to go back to academia."

He had often thought about what he would do instead of academic research. He could apply for a job with a larger company. But it was not easy to get a first job with no industry experience. There were a lot of unemployed scientists around. And how would a failed start-up look on a CV?

"Where is Broccaz?"

"Why do you ask me?" Tanya retorted, folding her arms.

"You speak with him regularly."

Martin tried hard to pick up any inadvertently revealing movements, but Tanya remained calm. "I don't speak with him any more than you do," she said.

Martin knew this wasn't true, but he didn't know how to challenge her.

"Why don't you just call him?" she continued.

"Well, I'm actually happy that he's left me alone the whole of last week. But that in itself is quite strange."

"Come on. He could be on vacation or on a business trip. He probably has many irons in the fire."

In a quieter tone of voice she said, "Martin, I'm starting to worry about you. Sometimes, you're behaving … how shall I put it … a little strangely."

Tanya reached out to touch his elbow. The sudden movement made him flinch. Tanya instinctively released his arm.

"What's going on? You're so … mistrustful."

He was glad that Tanya had avoided the word paranoid. When you become paranoid then you are no longer a natural sceptic, you are mentally ill. Walking in the street the other day he had noticed, on the wall of an underpass, something that normally would have made him smile, but instead it had saddened him. It was a graffiti: *'I am schizophrenic'*. Underneath someone had written *'That makes four of us'* in a different colour. Why couldn't he laugh at that? Was he beginning to lose his sense of humour?

"Well, you hit the friggin' nail on the head!" Martin snapped back. "Everything could go wrong now. I'm just on my guard!"

Tanya looked at him in silence for a few seconds.

"I'm just concerned about you," she said quietly. "That's all."

"Good. Don't worry, I am absolutely fine. Let's leave it at that, okay?"

Why could she not sense that something was not right? Was she pretending or was the whole thing a figment of his imagination? Something was definitely not right.

They went on to discuss the situation with the investors. Martin made her listen to the recording from Norbert Regenhofer from Upfront Ventures who ended his message with a suggestion that they meet at the Beau Rivage Palace Café. He would call Norbert Regenhofer later in the morning to set up the meeting and hoped this would not end in another beating-about-the-bush encounter.

As he opened a string of e-mails, his mobile phone started to beep continuously. It was not a call, but a signal warning him that the batteries were running low. Hadn't he just recharged it only two days ago? The phone was new and supposed to last for a week on every recharge. The few calls he had made were hardly enough to empty it this rapidly.

He decided to speculate about the possible reasons later. Perhaps it was just a reflection of his current condition, like a black hole, draining all his energy. But he was certain of one thing: this obscure thing in the dark, whatever it was, would not go away by itself.

17

One of the offices of Life Technology Ventures looked as if an atomic paper-bomb had ripped right through it. Fall-outs of sheets, stacks of paper and snippets of notes were spread all over the floor.

Kohler was sitting quietly in the epicentre on a chair. His colleagues went by the open door, some of them shaking their heads in amusement. Whenever an important decision had to be taken, Kohler preferred to sit down right in the middle of the information and let it gradually seep into his photographic memory.

He had sought out the most relevant articles and scientific reviews addressing one of the most important diseases of modern times. The meeting with Martin and Tanya had been the trigger. He wanted to get up to date on the complexities of cancer, though he fully realized that no one person could know all there was to know about existing and innovative treatment approaches.

There was an interesting historical overview on cancer therapeutics. World War II had marked the start of modern chemotherapy. The US army had conducted a clinical trial to develop protective measures against nitrogen mustard gas, a chemical warfare agent that caused severe skin burns. In the course of their investigations, they discovered a curious side-effect. The mustard gas had shown substantial activity against cancer in the lymph nodes. That marked the birth of alkylating agents, which introduced chemical changes to the DNA and thereby interfered with the DNA replication of growing cells. At the present time, Cyclophosphamide, a nitrogen mustard analogue, still remained one of the most important elements in many chemotherapy cocktails.

Kohler leaned back in his chair and looked through the haziness of the heavy sky behind the window. It was ripe for another monster thunderstorm. Who would have thought of mustard gas against cancer? Yet someone had discovered it.

He swung round and picked up another article from the floor, this time about Richard Nixon signing the US National Cancer Act on December 23, 1971 making the "conquest of cancer" a national crusade. The goal was simple and ambitious in line with other US war declarations: *Elimination of cancer*. What else could be as noble and ultimate as freeing the world from another major evil? Nixon expressed the hope that future generations would look back on it as the most significant action taken during his Administration.

How can you win a war when you don't even know who your enemy is? Kohler thought. Nixon couldn't have been further away from a quick victory. Today, more than thirty years on, the battle was raging as fiercely as ever – and cancer was still the clear winner.

The air conditioning emitted a low, growling whirr. It was working overtime like the rest of the office, even now at the beginning of October. Kohler tiptoed over to the oak desk, drank a large sip of mineral water from a green plastic bottle and went back to the floor.

He thought about the time when he was a young medical student. He had participated in several healthy-volunteer trials. Five hundred Swiss francs in return for ingesting a few pills had come in handy for supporting his otherwise penniless life-style.

It had been the best time of his life. No doubt about it. A feisty existence with nothing to lose and no obligations.

The interest in healing patients had always been there. Already as a ten-year-old he had wandered around with a house doctor's book, confidently diagnosing the measles of his younger brother before the family doctor confirmed it. By the time he turned twelve, he could remember most of the book by heart.

It was not only the treatment of patients that attracted Kohler to the medical profession. Disease itself fascinated him. The strange state of abnormality, the potholed skin textures, the ginger-root look of an arthritic finger, the odd colour shades of the whites of eyes. He was amazed at how the human body, made up of almost an identical set of genes, could present such an infinite number of variations.

He had practised as a doctor for five years, specializing in endocrinology. From time to time he wondered exactly why he had made the dramatic shift from medicine to finance. Was it the dehumanising, slightly demented and often brutal process of medical training that had taken its toll? Was it the intense pressure and chronic exhaustion of the doctor-to-be? Did he end up having his fill of treating ill patients day and night? Or had he just seen all there was to see?

He didn't know, despite the fact that he often thought about that crucial moment in his career, the point of no return, when he had decided to join a venture capital group. The day he and the bow-tied Grimau had agreed to join up together as partners over a three-star Michelin lunch.

Kohler grabbed another article from the office floor. It was about more recent cancer therapies. Drugs that starved the cancers by breaking down their blood supply. Other drugs that would direct the patient's own immune system to fight the cancer cells better.

Suddenly the telephone rang. Kohler looked at the screen of the cordless phone to see who it was. It read *'Caller*

ID anonymous' so he dumped it straight to the answering machine.

"Hello, this is Antonio Moretti, the CEO of Aldebaran. Just wanted to hear if you've received the business plan we sent you last week. Made some great progress with our transdermal drug delivery platform technology. Could make all your portfolio companies more competitive ..." The somewhat conceited entrepreneur paused. "Since I have tried to call you several times, I suggest you call me back between two and three this afternoon ... otherwise I might go to other VCs."

Sure. Can't wait to call you after you filled up my phone with a dozen voicemails, Kohler thought. *Aldebaran. Isn't that a star or something?*

The answering machine stopped recording and Kohler called his assistant.

"Louisa. That bloke from Aldebaran calls me day and night. Why on earth do you give out my direct number to people I don't know?"

"I'm sorry about that. He behaved like he knew you well."

"Stalkers are experts at that. Probably even knows the name of my dog. We do invest in people, but not in raving madmen and bleeding edge technologies. Get a standard rejection letter ready for him and I'll come and sign it."

"There are three other messages for you."

"Tell people to wait until this afternoon."

Annoyed by the interruption, Kohler turned his attention to an article on drugs targeting the dysfunctional telomer 'life-clock' of cancer cells. Instead of dividing about ninety times as a normal cell does, cancer cells switch off the clock and become immortal. Interfering with the dysfunctional telomer clock was a daring approach and could bring a lot of nasty surprises.

Kohler knew there would be no easy solution for dealing with cancer effectively, but there were approaches he liked more than others. Attis Therapeutics' strategy of targeting cancer stem cells was very promising, but also risky. He was certain that this would become an important event in cancer therapy. The question was, when? Antibodies disappointed in the early nineties – and then came back with huge success ten years later.

The experts had given a preliminary thumbs-up for Attis, so the only two items blocking a forward move were confirmatory lab data and the need to find one other investor who would be willing, and able, to co-lead the investment round.

18

Drugged with morphine to keep the intense pain at bay, Menarti was resting in the spacious bed of a small chalet above a gently sloping mountainside meadow, surrounded by a dense private forest that stretched as far as the eye could see. The dark green shutters of the chalet were open and flowerpots underneath each window spilled over with innocuous red geraniums. Vines, pleasing to the eye, climbed over the timbered natural larchwood, leathery brown after many years in the sun. Six other tiny chalets, their similarly delightful construction harmonizing with the graceful landscape, were scattered around the grounds and joined up with the main building, an old renovated farmhouse with winding gravel-covered paths.

Oddly enough, Menarti had no idea where he was. He had the impression that the silent young chauffeur who had picked him up at home two days before, had purposely made him lose his bearings by taking him on a long detour in order to tire him out. All along, his mind had floated in a constant mist.

This place was probably located in the Valais, but he could be wrong, it could be further north. The two nurses attending to him spoke impeccable French. Questioning them had been useless. Enquiries about the clinic and its practices were neither appreciated nor part of the arrangement. Not that it mattered anyway. The only thing he knew about the clinic, hidden away

from the prying eyes of the public, was its referral name: *The Swan.*
He was too exhausted to try to find out how it got that epithet.

Menarti turned in his bed and thought of all the hell he had had to go through during the past months. Aggressive chemotherapy had deteriorated his body in what seemed a fast-forward leap in time. He was down to fifty kilos and the few strands of hair that were left seemed ever more white. Even his paper-like skin appeared grey. A second CT scan had revealed more infiltrations in the stomach with the cancer turning more virulent from its location in the pancreatic tail. The surgeons had performed a diagnostic laparoscopy and discovered several metastases. The liver also had lesions that were biopsied as malignant.

Since the disease had been judged too widespread, the centre for cancer therapy back in Lausanne had chosen to end Menarti's chemotherapy and initiate merely palliative treatment. In a private conversation with Menarti's wife, the head oncologist had predicted that Menarti would live for only another two or three months.

Then a friend of a friend had told him about one last possibility.

He had been allowed in to the Swan clinic with the blessing of three members of the tightly-knit network and, last but not least, thanks to a hefty six-digit price tag, which did not even guarantee a successful outcome.

Despite feeling very weak when he arrived, Menarti could not be anything but surprised about the place. The staff seemed to be so few in number and only half a dozen cars were parked outside, in the shade of the pine trees behind the fenced entrance.

From the main building, they had transported him to his chalet through a maze of underground corridors, finally using a lift to get to his bedroom. The uncompromising and yet surprising beauty of the grey concrete that was to be found everywhere underneath made a fascinating contrast with the idyllic wooden exterior.

Three floors below the neatly manicured lawn of the Swan clinic, in a large sterile room, massive pipetting robots in the Class 100 clean zone were silently conducting thousands of experiments in parallel on high throughput assays containing fractions of Menarti's cells and tissues. Connected to each assay, dozens of spectrophotometers were detecting the slightest changes in cell behaviour, following each of the experiments. A state-of-the-art bio-simulator was masterminding it all by controlling the robots while it ran various mathematical cluster models to make sense of the immense amount of data, instantly designing new experiments, concurrently taking Menarti's physiological data, unwanted drug-drug interactions and many other factors into account.

Next to the physiological tests, specialists had scanned and analysed most of his body to define the boundaries of the first therapeutic course of treatment. In the race against the rapidly spreading tumour in Menarti's body, the aim was to find the optimal combination of drugs and their dosage to provide the most effective therapeutic treatment, designed specifically for him.

From a large and unique library of compounds in the underground Swan research laboratory, more than two hundred and fifty substances had been selected for testing in various combinations and at different dose levels. Some of the substances were used routinely in normal cancer practice at most hospitals. The majority, however, had never been tested on humans or in some cases not even on animals. An important role of the biosimulator was to minimize the risks of using these unknown compounds directly on ill human beings.

The task of the clinic was equally clear: to provide its personalized medicine, the only one of its kind, for a closed circle of terminal cancer sufferers from all over the world while keeping its practices out of sight from any nosy regulatory authorities and patent attorneys.

For the past eighteen years, the Swan clinic had successfully remained a well-hidden secret due to the strict banning of any visitors and extremely limited contact with the outside world. Patients were easily sworn to secrecy – after all, their very lives were at stake.

19

"Great that you could both come at such short notice," Norbert Regenhofer said as he motioned Martin and Tanya to one of the low tables in front of the Beau Rivage Café. The October afternoon sun still had sufficient strength to allow people to sit outside. The very tall partner of Upfront Ventures appeared to be in his late thirties and had a ruddy complexion. In one hasty, slightly awkward move, he sat down and pushed his knees to the side in order to avoid hitting the table.

"Sorry we're a bit late, Mr Regenhofer," Martin said, still short of breath from running, sensing the uncomfortable sweat between his spine and his shirt. Inside the parking area of the hotel, Martin had desperately looked for a spot, but the whole garage was full and every car seemed to be stuck firmly to its place. He eventually had to park some distance away from the hotel premises.

"Oh, don't worry about that. And please, call me Norbert."

Norbert made a ten-minute pitch on Upfront Ventures and his own credentials. As a drug developer, he had worked for two start-ups, one of which had made a lukewarm entry on the German stock exchange before it was merged with another biotech company in France. He didn't say what had happened to the other company.

Next to reading the Attis business plan, Norbert had studied a scientific article on Martin and Tanya's discoveries and had discussed this with several leading cancer experts who seemed to like the approach. Three days ago, he had obtained the green light from his board to move forward.

"So here's the deal," Norbert said. "At the beginning of next week, you will receive a first term sheet proposal from us. To gain time, I suggest that we negotiate the deal in parallel with the *due diligence* where we will make a thorough assessment of all aspects of Attis Therapeutics."

Martin nodded thoughtfully. "What investment amounts are we talking about?"

Norbert first looked at Tanya, then at Martin. "Two million Euros. A little over three million Swiss francs."

Martin tried hard not to betray his feelings. *Cash for over almost a year and a half!* Right now, that was forever.

"And how much of the company do you want for that?"

Tanya also played the indifference game to perfection.

"I'd prefer to let you know by Friday. But I can say that we usually let the founders keep the majority of the company in the first round."

Martin quickly calculated that his and Tanya's equity stake in Attis Therapeutics would be worth over one million Swiss francs each – at least on paper! Even his father would never have seen that kind of money.

"Do you need other investors for doing this deal?" he said.

"No. As opposed to most other investors, we're not afraid to invest on our own."

"That could potentially be of interest to us, but Tanya and I need to talk about this." Martin looked down, avoiding eye contact.

"Fine. Sleep on it," Norbert said. "I don't want to push you. But I would need some indication of interest by the end of next week. My first choice would be Attis, but I also have to decide on some other opportunities."

"We'll give you an answer before then," Tanya said firmly.

"Just one thing." Norbert stabbed a big dark olive with a toothpick. "In this financing round, we actually may insist on investing alone. For the next rounds we're open to invite other VCs in."

"That's quite unusual. I thought most investors would want to share risks," Martin said.

"In our field of expertise, I think we can manage that quite well. Other VCs tend to slow everything down as you probably have witnessed. That's not good when things are just beginning."

Norbert checked his electronic agenda and tapped on the screen with a small plastic stylus. "I need to rush off now," he said and stood up with a sudden, slightly uncoordinated movement.

"I have really enjoyed meeting both of you. I think we could probably make a deal within a month or so. I suppose that's not unimportant to you."

Back in the lab, Martin and Tanya debriefed their meeting with Norbert Regenhofer. They were both thrilled at the prospect of their first investor actually coming forward. Obtaining three million Swiss francs so rapidly would be great. It was not the ten million they originally had planned for, but significant milestones could be reached with the money.

Norbert's straightforwardness was appealing, but since he was after all a venture capitalist, some of it was probably an act. Then again, they doubted if any of these VCs could be trusted. With two-to-three months of cash in their bank account, Attis Therapeutics was rapidly running out of options. In addition, Broccaz had announced, much to Martin's and Tanya's dismay, that he was not willing to go on financing Attis, except perhaps to the extent of providing a small bridge-loan in the event that another investor was firmly on track to sign an agreement.

Gradually Martin came to the conclusion that Upfront Ventures probably was their best chance. The other investors were sitting on the fence, almost certainly waiting to pick up the bits and pieces to feed their floundering portfolio companies in case Attis had to be shut down.

Later in the afternoon, he made several phone calls to get advice from coaches and consultants. The consensus was that, in the current difficult investment climate for early stage start-ups, anyone lucky enough to attract money at decent rates should just go for it. A bird in the hand was worth two in the bush. Even Broccaz bought into that strategy with surprisingly little resistance.

20

The day after the meeting with Norbert Regenhofer, Martin had a long telephone conversation with Gavin who urged him to apply some pressure, gentle of course, on the remaining VCs to get them out of the woodwork. As Martin got on the phone to the VCs, one after the other baulked at the opportunity in a surprisingly unanimous way. In the space of a single afternoon, three VCs had politely declined by e-mail.

Martin was shell-shocked.

Yesterday's ecstasy after Regenhofer's promises was quickly replaced by deep uneasiness. Was there a fundamental problem with Attis? No straight answer was given by the VCs, just some vague statement that the opportunity did not fit in with their current investment strategy. So why did it fit in two months ago?

Martin was fuming. If ever this financing round worked out, he would make sure they would remain on the blacklist for any future rounds.

Kohler from Life Technology Ventures was the only investor who kept the discussion going, though he clearly was annoyed by the news that Upfront Ventures was the fast moving new kid on the block and that Regenhofer seemingly wanted to do the deal alone.

After a significant amount of internal arm-twisting, Kohler had obtained a consensus to move forward with Attis and was in the process of contacting potential co-lead investors that would carry out the full due diligence along with Life Technology Ventures.

Kohler did not know Upfront Ventures since this was the first time they had surfaced in Switzerland. He cautioned against working with people who were making their first investments in a new area, be it technology-wise or geographical, and mentioned the risks that going alone with a small fund could entail.

After many months stuck in the doldrums, Martin had never expected a piece of good news to create so much hassle and extra stress.

The big problem was the timing. Kohler said that Life Technology Ventures could not possibly make a compromise in its due diligence and internal deal-making process. Perhaps it could be done in three months, but one month was out of the question. Kohler would try to contact Norbert Regenhofer to find out what could be done.

After their discussion, Martin was very disappointed. He had honestly hoped that Kohler would invest; yet he had always wondered if it would really happen. Would Kohler just let go like the other VCs or would Martin finally be able to hook up with Life Technology Ventures?

It was late in the afternoon and Martin felt his head aching from all the phone calls and the constraints. Fabienne, the only lab technician still at work, came into the office. In just two months, she had made incredible progress in her work. Martin had been impressed with her professionalism in handling the lab procedures. She would ask for advice much more often and Martin had told her to inform him of any irregularity, however slight, before she told anyone else.

"Martin, do you have a minute?"

"Of course, what's up?"

"Remember that mycoplasma infection in the tumour cell lines?"

"I certainly do. That probably cut a year off my life expectancy."

Fabienne smiled uncomfortably.

Martin reached out and put a hand on her shoulder.

"Sorry, Fabienne. Forget what I just said." He looked her straight in the eye. "That's history now. It could have happened to anyone and I partly blame myself for not having put in those procedures before."

"Well. Yesterday, I was tidying up in one of the lab cupboards and found some of the old lab notes." She held up a block of squared paper.

"And?"

"Remember we thought the mycoplasma came from cross contamination?"

"You didn't check, I remember."

"Well I found out that I was the first one to use the laminar flow hood that day and that it had been cleaned the evening before."

"So the hood was clean." Martin said. "What's your point?"

"We thought the problem came from the cell lines. Both the cell lines were ok."

"You said you didn't check them."

"I didn't, but there are some notes here from Mireille who used them for another experiment. I spoke to her. Both cell lines had tested negative for infection."

"No kidding," Martin said, scratching his head. He mostly wanted that event buried and forgotten. "Where the hell did that Mycoplasma come from then?"

"Perhaps–"

A sharp screeching metallic sound ripped through the lab just before a deafening explosion shook the walls and windows all the way into the office where Martin and Fabienne were sitting.

Something very heavy rumbled across the lab floor, sounding like a huge bowling ball. It thudded against a wall that seemed to give in. Falling bricks could be heard.

The sound of a large piece of metal rotating lingered on for a little while, then everything turned silent – the longest seconds Martin had ever experienced.

Fabienne was in a state of shock, unable to speak or move. Martin had pulled her down with him as he dived to the floor. Through his hand, he felt her pulse beating fast through the thin skin of her neck.

He remained immobile for a moment, then slowly stood up. The shock wave had loosened several flakes of plaster from the office ceiling. One of them had fallen on the desk.

Martin bent down, thoughts racing through his mind.

"You … ok?"

Fabienne was still crouched on the floor and turned her pale face upwards.

"I … I … think so," she said. "My God! What's happening?"

"I've … no idea." Martin said in a state of stupor.

"Do you think it's safe?"

She stood up and looked around, noticing people staring with curiosity from the windows of the building opposite, confirming that something bad really had taken place.

"Perhaps it's not over. Come on. Let's get out of here and call the fire brigade."

"You can be sure they're already on their way." Martin just stood there, shaking his head. "It just can't be true. Not here. Not now."

He started walking towards the door. "I need to see what it is."

"Martin! Don't! There are chemicals in there. Another explosion could happen."

"This is too much. Too much ..."

Martin walked slowly through the corridor almost as though he were in a trance and entered the open laboratory.

The sight was horrendous.

Half of the lab was smashed to pieces. Several of the lab benches looked badly damaged and pieces of glass were lying all over the floor. Nasty-smelling chemicals had run out of their broken bottles and mixed with one another. Metal shrapnel stuck out of walls everywhere and the windows were gone. Martin looked at one of the HPLC machines that had fallen to the floor.

Fabienne came into the lab.

"Good God!"

Martin was speechless.

A huge hole in the wall and a device in front of it revealed what had happened: the rotor in the ultracentrifuge, used for separating biological components in small sample tubes, had gone berserk with a G force of half a million, breaking through the metal casing of the centrifuge as if it were a piece of paper.

Martin picked up the rotor, completely torn out of shape. Next to it on the floor was a piece of a printed circuit board. He looked up at the ceiling.

Whoever you are up there, why do you let these things happen? Is there some bad spell on me? Why? Dammit! Why?!

Minutes later, before the emergency services arrived, two police officers entered the lab and began to question Fabienne and Martin thoroughly. One of the policemen, who clearly had no idea what had happened, moved nervously about as if he were witnessing the first dramatic event of his professional career.

Martin hung his lab coat on the hanger in the corridor. Another challenge had been added to his struggle. Fair or unfair. He didn't give a damn anymore. Only one thing counted: getting a deal signed with the investors.

21

On the day of the centrifuge blast, Martin spent most of his time finalizing the reports for the insurance companies. The damage was extensive and the laboratory would have to be closed for at least three weeks for clean-up and repairs. Meanwhile, they would have to find other facilities to continue. Fortunately, the vials of protein drug were in a freezer outside the lab, but the laminar flow hood had been damaged and the fate of the cell cultures was uncertain. The new HPLC machine had not been blown off the bench and it seemed to work properly.

A representative from the manufacturers of the ultracentrifuge had come by. Everything pointed towards a very unfortunate accident. The possible causes were metal fatigue, perhaps caused by chemical corrosion, or imbalanced loading of the centrifuge, but Fabienne was certain that she had inserted an equal number of tubes facing one another. The device was old, granted, but it had been serviced impeccably. The representative finally left with the rotor wrapped up in a newspaper, taking it away for further examination.

Martin called Tanya, who was attending a European stem cell conference in Cracow in Poland. She was shocked by the news and said she would break off the conference and find a way to return by train as quickly as possible. He called Broccaz too, but could not reach him. That inquisitive man had been around every other day for weeks, so where was he now?

In the midst of Martin's pressing duties, the term sheet proposal from Upfront Ventures arrived by e-mail. It was difficult to be happy under such circumstances. In his short reply to Norbert Regenhofer, Martin downplayed the mishap, afraid of destroying all remaining hope for a financing round. During the negotiations, he would be obliged to tell them the whole story, unless of course, a miracle happened and a new lab became available quickly.

Strangely enough, the accident also provided a bit of relief. For some reason, Martin had come to dislike the place. And the mycoplasma appearance was now unexplained. Could there be a link? Could someone have sabotaged the ultracentrifuge in such a way that it looked like an accident? The idea seemed far-fetched. He could not think of anybody who would benefit from such acts.

The next day, Martin went to see Gavin about the term sheet from Upfront Ventures. He enjoyed coming to this piece of heaven where he could relax a little and share the burden of his responsibilities.

"Now, why am I not just a wee bit surprised?" Gavin roared as he studied the term sheet proposal through his rectangular-shaped reading glasses. They sat together in the quiet unlit library.

"What else could you expect from these guys!"

Gavin looked older with his glasses on; they didn't really fit him well. He had put off getting them for a long time, but the gradual progress of presbyopia had prevailed. He seemed to be in a generation of his own. Somewhere midway between Martin's father and grandfather. Old-fashioned, yet up to date – though contact lenses were clearly not an option.

Without saying a word, Martin watched Gavin, taking pleasure in every second they were together without Lindsey and Lorne. He could hear the logs crackling happily in the fireplace.

"This is nothing less than modern-day slavery!" Gavin scoffed with a voice rising towards gale force.

"Slavery?"

Gavin's eyes appeared just over the rims of his reading glasses. The wrinkles on his forehead deepened.

"They basically take the shares you already own in the company away from you. Then you can earn them back over a four-year period. It's called *vesting*. Very similar to the serfs in Medieval Europe who were bound to their land. The difference is that you have no lord of the manor to offer you protection in return. You get nothing from these people, except the honour of carrying all the risks. Boy, they really make me mad!"

"The investors say they want me to remain with the company."

"Perhaps. But if you leave the company *'with or without cause'* as it says right here, you'll lose the remaining unvested shares. In theory they could fire you after six months and keep all your shares."

"They'd have to pay for them."

"Yes. But only the nominal price, which is one Swiss franc per share. With the valuation they've put on the company, these shares are worth about forty Swiss francs each today."

"What do you suggest?"

"Get this term out of the agreement. In my opinion, this is a clear deal-killer. And there are several other things I really don't like."

Gavin the businessman was alive and kicking and had confirmed a key issue that a start-up coach had raised. From across the table, Martin could sense his intensity.

"Oh, I'd just love to challenge these VC guys face to face," Gavin said.

Martin smiled, looking at the wall where five daggers hung in a fan-shape. He pictured a ferocious encounter between Sir Gavin and Norbert the Gangly.

"Like this *'full ratchet anti-dilution'* clause. Really dodgy." Gavin took a hasty sip of his milk-filled afternoon tea. "Could make your ownership stake in the company evaporate like dew in the sun."

"I know. But I think the risk is slight. We will be creating a lot of value over the next year," Martin objected.

"Biology, like Nature, is not always predictable. I don't need to tell you that. Some of those milestones may take longer than you expect."

Martin thought of the numerous painful hiccups they had had in the lab.

Gavin looked at the document again. "If you miss a milestone and need money before it can be reached, then the anti-dilution clause may cause problems."

Despite never having been involved with VCs before, Gavin had pointed out many of the same crunch points as the start-up coach. The difference was Gavin's optimism on how much room for negotiation was left. He threw the four-page term sheet on the table and took his reading glasses off, placing them next to the teacup.

"There is something more important than everything else …"

"What is that?"

"Ninety percent of a typical contract deals with the situation when things go wrong," Gavin said. "And in this case the VC is putting a lot of risks on your shoulders. What you really want is a partnership where there is trust. Then, in most cases, the contract will never really need to be applied."

"What do you mean?"

"Do you trust them? Deep down in your guts, do you trust this Norbert Regenhofer?"

Martin rubbed his tired eyes.

"I have no idea. He seems to be the only one that moves forward, and so far he has delivered on his promises."

Gavin remained silent for a little while.

"Okay. You may be surprised to hear this from me, Martin, but I believe that gut feeling is one of the most important human assets in business. It helped me sell my company at the right moment to the right people. I had two offers. One appeared better on paper. It involved both cash and shares of the acquiring company. The other offer was cash only and it was twenty percent lower in total. Which one did I go for?"

"I suspect you went for the cash only deal." Martin said.

"Right. And you know why? Because I had this gut feel that the other company was hiding something. It was an American company and just three months later, it got heavily sued for improper marketing methods. Their share price plummeted."

"You were lucky."

"Call it luck, call it intuition. I think they're interrelated. You can analyse yourself to death with all the data that is available. With the Internet, *everything* can be found. Any opinion, right or wrong, is there somewhere. We can always find arguments against any decision. Take your start-up as an example. Why did you do it? If you analysed the pros and cons for doing a start-up, you'd probably never do it. But your gut feeling pushed you on, knowing that you would get something very valuable out of it. Am I right?"

Martin speculated on why he was so drawn to a world that at times could appear to be no more than sheer madness. Like a world parallel to real life with many of the same attributes, just much more intense and fast-moving. People trying to realize a dream in a world of unpredictability and unknowns, working crazy hours, sacrificing their personal lives, rushing along with all those other technology based start-ups. Medical devices, Internet search engines, telecommunications, nanotechnologies and all the rest competing for the same thing: *Money*. To make the realization clock tick a little faster.

"Funny you should say that," Martin finally said. "I've always thought of this start-up as a no-brainer. I never tried to justify it in any way. Except when I discuss it with my father. He's been against it from the very beginning."

"Your father probably has good reason."

"Of course. He wants me to take over the wine-making business."

"And you've never thought of doing it?"

"Not in my wildest dreams."

"Why not?"

"That's not the kind of life I want to live."

"What do you mean?"

"Not being in control. Having someone or something else control my destiny."

He told Gavin about an occasion when a fellow wine-grower had helped his father during a hailstorm, one of the nastiest enemies that in minutes can destroy many thousands of hard-worked hours by turning the most beautiful of fields into lines of naked bleak stems. His father had managed to ward off the threat at the last minute by firing anti-hail rockets into those suspicious-looking clouds as they approached. But a large part of the field towards the north was damaged anyway. And since Martin's father avoided insurance policies whenever he could, especially on the vines, the financial loss was devastating. Since then, his father had been trapped in bank loans on which he barely managed to pay back the interest each month. Nature had made his father a prisoner. From that day on, Martin had sworn to do whatever he could to avoid being dependent on anything. He would never become like his father. The biggest mistake in life was to let outside forces direct it.

"That's interesting," Gavin noted. "For someone who doesn't want external forces controlling his life, it's rather surprising to see you put everything in the hands of complete strangers."

Martin bit his lower lip. Although he had a deep respect for and affinity with Gavin, this remark annoyed him. Was this a subtle insinuation that he resembled his father anyway? Martin, the independent entrepreneur, who so badly wanted to avoid reproducing the habits of his father? He was certain that he had heard a trace of irony in the Scotsman's voice.

Gavin studied Martin in silence for a brief moment.

"It's funny," he then said, "how our discussion makes me think of my own business. I also wanted to be independent, my own boss, you know. That was my goal, more than anything else in my life. Pretty simple. And it happened the day I started my company. I considered myself successful on day one. In that sense, I was successful every day for the twenty-six years it lasted."

22

Kohler was furious. Earlier that afternoon, the investment committee of Life Technology Ventures had voted against his newest investment proposal, Attis Therapeutics. Arguably, of course, he had taken a risk by sticking his neck out for such an early-stage investment. But just like any other good entrepreneur, he was used to risks. Entrepreneurs do not like risks – contrary to common belief – they confront and deal with them to limit their damage potential.

Victor Grimau had made the scales tilt the other way. Until two days ago, Kohler was certain Grimau would back a deal on Attis. Today he had done the exact opposite. Suddenly, Grimau could see nothing but problems with the deal. And it was dreadfully evident who had planted the seeds.

Norbert Regenhofer from Upfront Ventures had only needed twenty minutes on the phone to persuade Grimau that Attis still carried tremendous risks. The list included unresolved questions regarding the protein manufacturing scale-up and its subsequent refolding into the correct three-dimensional protein structure. Regenhofer had pointed out that such work could pose headaches for years in the attempt to ensure high therapeutic efficacy. That meant a lot of tedious early-stage investigation work, best suited for a seed investor like Upfront Ventures, not for a larger investor like Life Technology Ventures.

Kohler realised that Regenhofer was playing his cards very smartly, knowing that a large fund such as Life Technology Ventures could not move rapidly. It was evident that Regenhofer wanted to do the deal on his own. The only way Kohler could get back in would be to convince the committee to approve a small investment, made in a very short time-frame, for keeping Martin and Tanya hooked.

That strategy had failed miserably with the vote against him today. He deeply regretted the decision of the committee and began thinking about the best way to inform Martin about the unfortunate outcome.

Tanya was doing a great job in putting the lab back together. With the help of the university administration, she had found most of the necessary glassware and equipment. For centrifuging, they were allowed to use the machine in the immunology department of the university a bit further down the street. In the lab, a fresh layer of plaster covered the big hole in the wall and the many small spots where the shrapnel had hit. Only one of the HPLC machines worked. Fortunately, they had enough therapeutic protein for the first toxicity studies.

Martin wondered if Regenhofer would still put three million on the table if he could see this lab looking as though it had been through a civil war. Well, in one week it would all be history, with the whole thing repainted.

The slim document on his desk in the lab office looked rather insignificant among the tall stacks of scientific articles. Martin repeatedly picked it up, flipped over to the signature page, looked at it for a few seconds and then put it down again. It was still hard to believe that he had obtained a term sheet from Regenhofer, signed for three million Swiss francs. Upfront Ventures now officially agreed to all the important conditions for the financing deal, a big step towards the final contract.

Martin looked at the papers again. It was all in there, in that document. All the pain and suffering he had gone through during the year.

Regenhofer was more flexible than Martin had hoped. After a few surprisingly painless negotiations, he and Tanya had managed to rid the term sheet of the nasty anti-dilution clause and the founder share-vesting scheme. The compromise was a slightly lower company valuation and a couple of other, rather small, concessions. Martin had been permanently on the phone with Gavin, Broccaz and numerous other advisors and coaches. In the end, everyone agreed that this would not be a bad deal at all. Several people, however, reminded Martin that a deal was not done until the final contract was signed, so he kept a lid on his excitement.

The telephone on Martin's desk rang. On the display, he could see that the call came from Life Technology Ventures.

"Martin, I'm afraid I have some bad news for you," Kohler said, somewhat distantly. "We have decided not to invest in Attis. I know this may come as a surprise to you, but under current circumstances we have to back out. We could not rush things as you wanted."

Martin wondered what *current circumstances* really meant, but refrained from asking. Clearly, things had not worked out between Regenhofer and Kohler. Probably another VC ego clash.

"I really didn't have a choice," Martin said, defensively. "We were running out of time with Attis."

"I see," Kohler said, not sounding truly convincing. "Well, I wish you all the best in your venture."

Disappointed, Martin hung up with the bizarre feeling that this would not be the end of their encounter. He really liked Kohler. With Regenhofer, it was different. He was the type of person you neither liked nor disliked. The telephone call had been somewhat of a cold shower and Martin did not feel great about it. But, life had to go on. Right now, money spoke louder than anything else.

I can give you a good recipe for failure and that is trying to please everybody. Gavin's words echoed in the back of Martin's mind. Ahead of him was a task beyond measure, the biggest challenge of his life so far. He knew he had to pull this one through on his own. Cool-headedness and rationality was the recipe.

The signed term sheet was his first little victory in a very long time. Martin wondered whom he could call at three in the afternoon. Someone not related to the lab and who could make him think of other things.

Unfortunately Sarah was busy working on a new landscaping project for an American company, setting up their facilities around Morges. Perhaps Tom would be free; they hadn't seen each other for the past two months.

Martin called the estate agency where his friend worked. The place sounded very busy and Tom had some serious last minute problems with the sale of a piece of land. Buyer and seller behaving like spoilt kids. Before hanging up though, Tom managed to give a detailed account of his new girlfriend, a redhaired little number from a fitness club in Ouchy. He had lost almost five kilos.

Martin took off the lab coat and made his habitual pocket search before hanging it up on a hook next to the other coats on the wall of the corridor. He knew what to do. He deserved a little walk through the town. Exercise was long overdue and he could buy some flowers for Sarah on the way – they too were long overdue.

23

The weather was breezy and a few scattered raindrops landed gently on Martin's face as he walked down the Rue du Bugnon. The slope of the street made him walk quickly and he took deep breaths to refresh his brain.

On top of the Bessières bridge, he stopped and glanced at the street below. He could see through the office windows that people were still at work; that gave him a strange sense of liberty. Disquieting, in a way, a bit like playing truant. Some bright red leaves on the pavement were whirling around. He suddenly sensed how cold the air had become. Autumn had sneaked in unnoticed, behind his back. Just like everything else.

He kept on walking in the light rain, trying to do some positive thinking. He was going to stay on the ball. Had he missed something with the deal?

Nothing came to mind. Hadn't they all agreed that this was a pretty good deal? Yet something was still nagging him. Why did he feel worried when there was nothing to be worried about? He did not like the way Kohler had pulled out of the deal, but what could he do about it?

He crossed the Riponne Square and entered a pedestrian street where an unkempt man with wild eyes and long dark greasy hair came up to him, asking for money. Martin ignored him as much as he possibly could and hurried past. At a red traffic light further on, he turned round and saw the man walking with an unsteady gait towards another pedestrian. The movements looked strikingly similar to those of Martin's uncle, a sufferer from multiple sclerosis. Why had he not seen that immediately? Martin rummaged in his wallet and found a five-franc coin. He hurried back to where he had seen the man, but the fellow was gone. Martin stopped and let out a sigh.

Could he not even manage to give beggar a few francs? It made him think of his own and Attis' finances. Why, all of a sudden, had the flow of money become so incredibly complicated?

Martin looked at his watch. He had been walking for half an hour. It felt more like two hours. The rain was coming down harder and he pulled up the hood of his coat. Back to reality. Flowers for Sarah.

He headed towards the flower shop he had visited all too seldom lately, picturing a charming autumn bouquet in russet shades. Sarah would be delighted. He would go on a little spending spree to please her today – and to please himself by getting some relief from all these money constraints.

A hand-written sign on the boutique *Bac-à-Fleurs* brought the unfortunate news that the shop was closed for the holidays. Martin cursed his bad luck. With the rain now pounding down, he would be soaked within five minutes. Instead of looking for another flower shop, he went into the shop next door, a small furniture outlet. *Why not just buy a new sofa instead?* Or anything else, just to spend money. To feel the energy of the transaction.

He walked through the shop, looking around and musing. *Darling, I couldn't get any flowers for you but I found this great new kitchen suite on the way home. You should have seen the look on the vendor's face when I said it was a gift and asked him to wrap it up.*

After five minutes, a vendor came towards him, but Martin had already turned round and was on his way out of the shop.

It was still raining hard outside and Martin hurried home feeling completely frustrated by the afternoon. Being tied up would not be his contribution to the world. It could not last forever. He knew he had things to do, but what? What were those small pieces accumulating in the inner recesses of his mind? And what was the restriction, the inexplicable plug that was holding everything back? His afternoon walk was supposed to clear his thinking. Well, to some extent it had: somehow, all his problems revolved around money.

Sarah was still at work when Martin called her from home around five o'clock. She would be home rather late, eight in the evening, perhaps even later. She told him not to waste time cooking; she would see to things when she got back home.

Martin saw a surprise dinner dissolving as well. He wandered about the flat with increasing irritation over the disintegrating afternoon. Why was everything going against him again? And now, Sarah working late? Sarah never worked late, except on very rare occasions when she would bring her work home. What was that all about?

Restless, he went into the kitchen, made some goat cheese sandwiches and took a beer out of the fridge. His brain was so distracted that he hardly noticed what his mouth was doing. He ate too quickly and too much. Could he really trust Sarah? Perhaps, but he would watch her more carefully from now on. And anyway, whom could he really trust?

The sky had turned black outside and the rain had stopped drumming on the roof over the bedroom where Martin had temporarily placed the desktop computer from the office. It was tempting to go through his e-mails, but with the bad luck he had had today, the mailbox would probably contain a stream of distressing news that would initiate a merciless destruction of the little that remained of his day.

He thought of Broccaz again. Could he have been behind the explosion? This fellow was definitely up to something else besides Attis, but what reason could he possibly have to blow up the lab of the company he had invested in? That made no sense at all. What about Tanya? Why was she so far away when the explosion happened?

A message bleeped in on his mobile phone and interrupted his train of thoughts. Sarah suggested that they meet at a café near the Cathedral.

An hour later Martin watched her arrive at their rendezvous. He was still not completely used to her new, shorter hairstyle; it made her look older.

Sarah kissed him. She grabbed his hand and they started walking.

"What if we skipped that drink?"

"Why? It was your idea." Martin resisted. "You love an occasional Margarita. What is all this? First the new hairdo. Now you don't like Margarita's."

"How about just … walking instead?"

"You're not hungry either?" Martin said. "What is wrong with *you*?"

She stopped.

"No. What's wrong with *you*? You almost sound like some kind of private investigator. I had my dinner from the office fruit basket, all right? Besides, I want to lose a couple of kilos. You've always been teasing me, saying I've got a bit of a tummy. So, let's walk."

They walked up the steps behind the Musée Cabinet des Médailles.

"You never work late at the office," Martin said grimly.

"You *always* work late."

"Not today."

"Too bad. You want me to be on stand-by for whenever you're free?"

"You know what I want?" Martin said. "I want someone to come up to me, just once, and tap me on the shoulder, and say: '*Hey Martin, you know what? You're doing pretty ok. Things will be all right.*'"

"And you think I haven't done that?" Sarah exclaimed. "But when someone walks towards the edge of a cliff, distracted by watching birds in the air, do you still want me to say: '*You're doing great, just keep going straight on!*'"

"You don't understand."

"Martin. I am worried about you. You've got to change now before it's too late. There is a life beyond Attis."

"Three more months. That's all I'm asking for."

Sarah paused.

"Do you ever dream of me?"

Martin's stare went on infinite. "I try to. But I can't."

"What do you dream of then?"

"I make wishes instead."

"Wishes? About what?"

"That I don't want to be disappointed in myself."

"And what about us, Martin? Shouldn't we make wishes for *us*?"

"Of course. It's just … all these things that are going on. Some of it is quite strange. I have issues that never leave me in peace."

"Then tell me about them. Why have you stopped telling me about what's going on with Attis?"

"I'm too tired when I get home. I prefer to keep things separate. Business and private life. Otherwise I won't make it."

"What private life? There is nothing left of it."

Martin remained silent, then said, "I think we should stop talking about work, Sarah."

"This is not about work. It's about you. Your health. Is it really worth it?"

He did not answer.

Why do women always get into a relationship with men in the hope of changing them? Martin thought. *Men are different. Men engage with women in the hope they will not change too much.*

"Then, at least, give me a kiss instead," she said, sounding a little sad.

He met her kiss, sensing the pleasantness of her. He kissed her back until there was nothing left except the taste of despair.

In silence, they continued their walk, each in their thoughts. Martin could feel that tiny place on his skin, on the right side of his face, just above his lips, where Sarah had left a teardrop.

This evening was so different from the one last year when they had walked the same paved streets around the cathedral. When they had heard the Town Crier shouting out the hour from the four sides of the South tower of the Cathedral.

'C'EST LE GUET ... IL A SONNÉ MINUIT!'

It had been such a magic walk. He had felt a never-ending delight whenever she asked him to warm her hands. He loved sensing the fresh coolness and the soft skin of those fine fingers against his. At the time, it had struck him how easy it would be. The perfect place. He could just continue holding her hands on the lantern-lit cobblestones, kneel down in front of her and pop the question. But the moment had not been right.

That evening, a year ago, he had made a firm promise to himself: the next time they came here, he would do it. He would put into words the question he so fervently wanted to ask her.

The next time they came here.

24

S till confined to one of the chalets at the Swan clinic, Menarti slowly rolled over to the left of the wide wooden bed and carefully swung his feet down on to the floor. Standing up meant great pain, but he grabbed his crutches and shuffled with short unsteady steps towards the door to the balcony. Although he had lost a lot of muscle force, his limbs had little weight to carry. He passed the wash-hand basin on the way to the glass door and pulled the curtains aside. Fresh cold air met him as he opened the door; he breathed in a lungful. It had a pleasant crispness to it, plus that sweet earthy smell of newly fallen rain.

Six different drugs were combined in the first treatment, which had been the worst. It had been carefully tailored with the help of the bio-simulator and the high-throughput automated clonogenic lab in the basement. In one week, the robots had performed experiments that roughly equalled ten man-years of work.

Never in his life had Menarti experienced such excruciating pain, sweeping through every single synapse, breaking through the high doses of morphine in his bloodstream. The cancer had to be hit as hard as possible because it had become very virulent and resistant to standard chemotherapy.

They had not lied to him about how awful it was going to be. His whole body felt as if it had been set on fire from the inside. It had lasted for two hours and he had eventually passed out.

He faintly remembered the all-consuming feeling of death just before it happened. After that horrible turning point, he was now certain that he had come back to life.

In the weeks that followed the first course of treatment, Menarti received another two different types of drug cocktails. Each of those, too, was painful but he suffered less, exactly as they had told him. His initial concern over the anonymous compounds entering his body was wiped away by his growing faith in the expertise of the bio-simulator, imitating and learning about his body all the time. By now, it knew infinitely more about his personal metastatic pancreatic cancer than the world's best oncologists would ever be able to comprehend.

Within minutes, Menarti's fragile body started to shiver from the air coming across the balcony; he closed the glass door. Life had stretched out its hand to him again. He had a very real chance of survival; the next few weeks would tell whether things were on the right track. He was eager to phone his wife and tell her the encouraging news.

25

$\mathbf{M}$artin had little else to do but wait. The week had seemed long and on several occasions, he found himself daydreaming about the future of Attis. Milestones being met, partnerships with pharmaceutical companies being created, more rounds of financing, articles in the newspapers, and finally – the entry on a public stock exchange that would send everyone to financial heaven.

With Upfront Ventures, the road from the term sheet to the final agreement had been a relatively smooth ride. This week, Regenhofer's lawyer was doing a last fine-tuning of the document.

Every morning at eight, Martin had rushed to the letter-box, hoping to find a big spine-tingling envelope. But again today, the box had disappointed him – just some ads, a free local newspaper and a couple of bills, one of which came from the commercial registry office in Berne.

Waiting was unbearable; Martin's impatience was stretched to the limit; he was again having difficulty sleeping at night. Just now, he felt slightly unsteady, wondering if he was experiencing the initial stages of the flu that had begun its pre-Christmas devastation in the region. At lunchtime, he would buy some aspirin and a bottle of extra-strong vitamins. He did not dare to phone Regenhofer, afraid of the negative impact that had followed his phone calls to the other investors. Instead, he zap-clicked impatiently through a web site concerning healthcare studies.

Martin thought of Kohler. He had replayed the sequence over and over again in his head: Kohler backing out from the deal as unexpectedly as lightning from a bright blue sky. Had Kohler even put up a fight with Regenhofer? Something had happened. Martin could not stop thinking about the possible reasons.

The sound of Fabienne moving around, cleaning pipettes and flasks, interrupted by the occasional nose-blowing, came from the corridor. She was the only technician left on the payroll, so as to keep the company burn rate at a minimum until the deal was done.

A faint growling noise caught Martin's attention. A fax was ticking in on Tanya's desk. With a mixture of fear and excitement, he ran over and almost tore the paper out of the fax machine. It carried the Upfront Ventures letterhead.

'... we very much regret to inform you that, for legal reasons which our own investors have brought to our attention and which are beyond our control, we are unable to move forward with any investment in Attis Therapeutics ...'

Martin read the paragraph a second time in sheer disbelief. He was still not sure that he had understood correctly. They were just words thrown together, disconnected and meaningless. Only after his third reading did the words 'regret' and 'unable' slowly begin to sink in. The sentence would make an indelible imprint on Martin's mind.

It couldn't be true.

The room started swirling; everything in it was swinging from side to side, making Martin too dizzy to move. He sensed his entire weight being pulled down on the chair. A paralysing force had taken hold of him and all he could hear were the rapid beats of his pulse, throbbing on his eardrums.

Close the deal, Martin. Close that bloody deal. Why didn't you go with Kohler? There's money for only two more months. Then it's over. No, the show isn't over till the fat lady sings, right? So, where's the fat lady? What do you mean, legal reasons? Shit! Regenhofer, you bastard, you saw it coming, didn't you?!

He closed his eyes and the grip loosened a little.

It just can't be bloody true! All the suffering. For what?! First Kohler and now Regenhofer. Are they all in this together in some kind of conspiracy?

"You okay?" Fabienne suddenly stood next to him.

"What?"

"You shouted."

"Did I?" Martin said from somewhere far away.

"You shouted *'Why?'*"

"I suppose I did."

"You've gone completely white. Are you sick?"

Martin looked at the fax again and anger started flaming up within him. Who the hell did they think they were, these VCs?

"It's over, Fabienne." Martin stared ahead. "Done, finished ..."

"What's happening?"

He was like in a trance.

"The last investor just pulled out. You can start preparing your CV for another job. We have to close Attis."

Fabienne was shocked.

"But I thought ..."

"We all thought," Martin interrupted. "Or rather – we all dreamed."

Fabicnne let out a long sigh.

"Yes. All this work for nothing," Martin said. "Attis was a great idea, but sometimes greatness just isn't good enough."

The telephone rang in Martin's office and he walked slowly out of the lab through the corridor. What was the point in picking up the telephone? It was over. It would all be history.

The phone kept ringing.

It was Tom.

"Did you see the newspapers today?" he asked excitedly.

"No. Why would I want to do that?"

"Jesus. You're really in a great mood. Okay, here's something to cheer you up."

"Tom, I'm not in–"

"I don't usually read much of the business stuff, but one of my colleagues does. There's a tremendous article on your company, Attis, in one of the local papers. Half a page on your technology and drugs, really well written."

"Thanks for the news Tom, but things are not going great here. Our last hope, a German investor, just dropped out."

"So, you still did not raise any money?"

"No."

"Oh, man. I'm sorry to hear that. Well, then, I guess the journalists must have got it all wrong then."

"What do you mean?"

"They said that you were just about to receive three million francs."

26

Dressed in a long-sleeved blue shirt, brown corduroy trousers and a pair of loafers, Emile Broccaz sat with his laptop computer and a cappuccino on the covered balcony of his flat within a stone's throw of the lake. Despite the unusually warm November weather, only a few boats had dared to venture out on the calm water.

He had finished skimming through the *Financial Times*. The stock market was recovering a little after some very tough months. Even this year would be another good money-earner for him. It rarely failed, that final quarter of the year, when the financial institutions were trying hard to make their numbers add up.

He emptied the cup, placed it on the table and clicked the 'sell' button on his on-line trading system, locking in two hundred thousand dollars of profits on the sale of put options in an IT company quoted on the Nasdaq.

Not that he cared much about money. He did not need all that much, living as he did on his own with rather modest expenditure. Money was the quantifiable proof of his exceptional calls and judgements. Nothing more. The luxurious flat was further proof. After twenty years in investment banking, he had retired early and did even better investing on his own, with ample freedom for other endeavours.

Perfection and control were the pillars of his success. He had learned it all the hard way when his mother died of colorectal cancer. She was still surprisingly young to catch that form of cancer and it was discovered too late, having spread to the lymph nodes.

The unspeakable despair he had felt watching her was forever chiselled into the depths of his conscience. Doctors acting in pure self-defence, covering their backs while she suffered. He could have killed them all, those incompetent fools. Blindly trying one treatment after another so that they could complete their checklist, with his mother as the tormented guinea pig.

When she died, something inside him died as well. At twenty-five years of age, he had lost faith in human beings. He swore never to experience that feeling of vulnerability again. What was a helpless human being? Nothing. Like his father, who couldn't cope with life and became an alcoholic.

Emile Broccaz became a master at everything he attempted. Martial arts, fencing and later on a university degree in economics. It was not the desire to win that drove him – it was the basic need to survive, the daily fight for life.

He worked desperately hard as an investment banker and when he turned forty, at a time when many people start asking themselves all kinds of foolish questions, he knew what his life was about. With his dedication, a unique project was to see the light of day: a cancer clinic offering the ultimate personalized medicine with custom designed drug therapies for each individual patient. The new approach would be totally devoid of flawed human intervention. There would be no need for doctors any longer – key decisions were all to be made by powerful expert systems.

He knew from the beginning that he could do it. Aware that the World was not ready to embrace such a radical paradigm shift, he had decided to go about it with a high level of discretion. And so, in all secrecy, inside an old isolated farmhouse standing on a vast area of land, he had begun the construction of the experimental cancer clinic that he later named the Swan clinic.

Today, eighteen years later, the clinic still looked rather insignificant from the outside, but the underground research capabilities had grown tremendously with state-of-the-art technology and, most recently, with modern methods for gathering information in the life science field.

For the past year, his computer experts had worked out an efficient way of tapping into new academic discoveries in their early stages, before they had been published or patented. The first test sites had worked remarkably well.

Through an innocent looking e-mail with a renowned journal as the apparent sender, any scientist clicking on the link would trigger an undetectable *spear phishing* attack that would give access to the entire network system to which the computer was connected.

Emile Broccaz had dubbed the venture *'Carnivore'*, inspired by an infamous FBI Internet surveillance project, now designated more innocently DCS1000. Carnivore was able to unbolt most doors to computers used by cancer researchers all over the world.

Targeting academic researchers was the key to the Carnivore project. The idea was to exploit the innate, almost naïve, willingness of scientists in academia for sharing information, as opposed to researchers in private companies. In addition, most radical innovations took place in academic laboratories. Pharmaceutical companies and even some of the larger biotech companies were all suffering badly from chronic incremental thinking.

Through Carnivore, Broccaz had the freedom to collect real-time data relating to a specific drug target, a biological pathway or classes of chemical compounds and proteins, before the data was published or patented. An instant tap into the limitless pool of biotechnology innovation.

There would be a tidal wave of data coming in. But Emile Broccaz knew exactly what to do with it. A very powerful computer would chew through the massive amounts of data and discover new universal truths before anyone else.

Yes, he could certainly be pleased with himself. He had found his mission in life and every breath he took tended towards that goal. A unique role had been offered him on this deficient planet; he had embraced it and was now carrying it out to perfection.

Broccaz picked up the laptop, logged on to a secure web-site and typed in a ten-digit mobile phone number. A detailed map appeared on the computer and a little triangle-shaped icon could be seen in the middle of the map. It moved very slowly, along what appeared to be a motorway next to a large blue speck of water. He could see that the phone was in use and clicked on the "open line" button. Through the speakers of the laptop came the sound of a car engine and two voices, one of which he knew very well.

"... it was a disaster. My father kept on reminding me of the many times he warned me about Attis. That it was too risky and would fail. I couldn't stand the sight of him. It was a bad idea to go visit my family. I really feel like crap. Sarah, I need to be with you. Let's just stay at home this afternoon."

27

A huge flock of birds flew over the yellow-red glowing wine fields. The thousand tiny dots formed a gigantic fingerprint, moving swiftly with sudden changes of direction in perfect synchronization. Abruptly, they all swooped down and flattened out into a black line, breaking up into two groups, each with its own one-dimensional life for a few seconds, then moving upwards to melt together again and create the initial shape of the flock. Pulsating movements, like a heart beating in slow motion, as the final exercise before a long and strenuous journey.

Tinged with sadness, Martin watched the birds through the window of his car as he drove back from the Valais. His father had been right after all. The foolish dream was over now. He had come back to the bitterness of reality.

The sight of rows of wine stems stirred up old images of the chalky smelling fields on his parents' estate. Endless lines of yellowing leaves and sweet berries flickered up from a sunny past. The tired, hurting fingers clinging to the cutlery around the dinner table. Everyone exhausted, but often in a good mood. And the brief moments when his parents laughed happily together, their cheeks reddened from too much sun and too much of their own white wine.

The tiredness he felt now was both physical and mind-numbing. The visit to his parents' place had been anything but sunny. After another restless night on sleeping pills, the effect of which gradually wore off, he had made an escape to see them. Not that it had done him any good. Martin's father had been quick to remind him that his help had been greatly missed at the *vendanges*, the annual grape-picking, which was a traditional family event. And all through the morning, his mother had stared at him with a terrified look that said: 'You look like a ghost, what's happening to you?'

'I was out really late last night,' he had lied. Better to be a party animal than a trauma wreck. He told them the bad news, but not about the consequences. His mood had continued its grim slide until he decided to leave them shortly after lunch; he could not bear their presence any longer. Mum treating him as if he were terminally ill and Dad scoffing in contempt. *I told you this was a stupid idea.*

He felt like a lonesome animal, lost and with no sense of direction, unaware of what might eventually happen. How painful it was to have people congratulating him about Attis after the newspaper article when he had to tell them that the whole thing was off.

Only one wish was on his mind: to disappear into the comfort zone of the flat and wait for things to get better. They could only get better.

When he entered the living room, Sarah was about to clear a spot on the wall to hang up a new poster.

"Why are you taking that painting down?" Martin grunted.

"I just think the old painting of that lighthouse doesn't fit in here any more. We need more colour."

"Please don't change it now. Can't we just leave things as they are?"

"I've been wanting to change it for months now. It's depressing."

"I don't want more colour. Not now."

"You said you liked this new poster."

"I'm tired of fucking arguing. Don't put that poster up now – *comprendes*?" Martin yelled and headed for the kitchen.

"Martin!" Sarah ran after him. "This has been going on for too long now. I don't recognize you any more."

"Right, whatever …" Martin opened the fridge and studied the contents.

"You have a serious burn-out or something like that. Why don't you get some help for coping with it. Some professional help."

"A shrink?!"

His head came shooting out of the fridge. "What the hell are you saying? That I'm mentally ill?"

"Of course not. I … I just don't know what to do."

"You know what kind of help I need right now? One million Swiss francs and you will see me happier than ever." He took a can of beer from the fridge and opened it.

"Can't you see that there's more to life than Attis?"

He took a large gulp from the can and opened a bag of popcorn.

"Don't want to talk about it right now, okay?" Then he walked to the living room and turned on the television.

"Yes you will." Sarah said, irritated. "Look at how much you've been drinking these past weeks." She hesitated for a moment. "Look what you're turning into. That's not the kind of man I want to marry."

"What? What's that supposed to mean? That I'm not good enough for you?" Martin said as he jumped up from the sofa.

"You're destroying yourself. And our relationship."

"Sure … just put all the blame on me. "

"When will you start listening?" she shouted. "Why are you always so damn … thick-headed?"

In a hazy moment of temper, the words not coming out as they were supposed to, his brain too worn out to think of new arguments, Martin came very close to slapping her, but he held back and yelled out some simple hard-hitting words at her instead.

Then things took a completely new turn.

Sarah made a quick telephone call, packed a small suitcase and left. Decided to move over to a girlfriend's.

Behind the slammed front door, Martin kept on shouting.

"One little problem and look who's taking the easy way out! Letting me down like everyone else, huh!"

Curled up on the sofa, still groggy from Sarah's departure, Martin tried to soothe his misery with popcorn, beer and Formula 1 racing. He watched the cars doing a couple of laps, but he could not keep his attention on the race. Let alone the corners Alonso was cutting.

Did he push her out? No, she was the one who had decided to leave. He still could not believe what had happened. Sarah running off like that? What if everyone bolted when they faced some trouble? What if he just did the same, running off from the mess at Attis?

He ate a plateful of dark chocolate to feed his craving. Alonso seemed to be having problems with the transmission.

The blend of chocolate and beer made him doze off while vivid and weird afternoon dreams rolled over him. In one, a huge chemical reaction was taking place. Millions of different molecules were circling round one another, making all sorts of movements. Rotating. Intertwining. Unwinding. In a split second, faces appeared on all of the molecules. He recognized none of them, yet they all appeared familiar. Millions of human beings reacting with one another in one massive chemical reaction, turning into new and bizarre structures.

In the middle of the dream, so amazingly genuine that he felt it going to the very marrow of his bones, Martin heard a mobile phone ringing. He tried to resist, but the intruding noise did everything it could to tear him away. He stood up and ran towards the coat hanger in the entrance. The ringing came from the pocket of his coat.

It was a sales rep from a wine import company with a new offer on a shipment of Burgundy red wine coming in. The man, obviously not from the French-speaking part of Switzerland, spoke exceedingly slowly and articulated as if ten-pound weights were dangling from his jaws.

"A *Château Mignon*. There are only eight cases left but I may be able–"

"No!"

"… to secure two cases for you. They are from the amazing year of 2000 and we also have them as Magnums which–"

"Hey!" Martin said.

"… there are only a few bottles left and–"

"STOP!" Martin yelled with a voice that almost cracked.

There was a brief silence. For a few moments, Martin believed he had been listening to a cassette player.

"You know what you can do for me?" Martin continued, softly.

"Tell me, sir!"

"You take that Château Migraine, right?"

"Er … No, the name of the–"

"… and shove it!"

A sharp intake of breath could be heard at the other end of the line and the person hung up. Martin felt relieved. At least one person, who did not – who could not – fight back. Now they had started calling people on their *mobile* phones to advertise their stuff! The disappointment that the caller was not Sarah had further added to his annoyance.

He let out a deep sigh, wishing he could just wipe out the past year and start again with a clean slate. There were so many things he would do differently. Now it was too late. The urge to patch up with Sarah to avoid whatever utterly loathsome existence was coming his way ran parallel to a powerful desire to be alone.

Martin spent the remainder of the day moving restlessly from one end of the flat to the other, mainly between the television set and the fridge. The phone rang several times, but he did not pick it up and he had disconnected the answering machine.

Unwashed dishes started to pile up. On the way through the corridor, he noticed that the whole flat was starting to get into a disorder. Clothes on chairs, articles and books on the floor, half-empty cans of beer, plates of unfinished food seemed slowly to invade the place. It stung his eyes. He hated mess, but he did not have the energy to do anything about it right now. Tomorrow. Tomorrow he would have a go at it. And begin to deal with the mess at Attis as well.

In the evening, when he could no longer bear the solitude and the quietness anymore, he dialled Denise's number, the friend with whom Sarah was going to stay, but all he got was her answering machine. A call to Sarah's mobile phone also turned out to be fruitless. He left her a short message.

Anger blazed up through him like wildfire.

Was Sarah looking at the caller identity screen right now? Letting him hang on and suffer just that little bit more. Perhaps she was sitting in a café with Denise, psychoanalysing him over a cup of herbal tea.

Martin grabbed a handful of popcorn and chewed on it frantically before flushing it all down with rapid gulps of beer from a half-empty can on the table. Anger and popcorn, all crushed together.

He would crush the problems out of himself. He was tough and would fight until the last drop of blood. He always had done so anyway, so why not now? Life was all about having the guts to fight back.

Martin suddenly felt overwhelmingly tired, uncertain whether he would be able to muster enough strength to put his thoughts into practice. But letting things go their own way was just not an option.

As all this churned through his mind, he bit extra hard on some popcorn and heard a crack. An excruciating pain shot all the way up through his head. He spat the contents of his mouth into his hand; one bit felt heavier than the rest. Something had given way. And this time it was not the popcorn. A big piece of a molar tooth stared upwards at him in contempt after a failed confrontation with a grain of maize.

He cursed himself. How could he have been stupid enough to chew on a maize grain? With the little resolution he had managed to mobilize, why was every damned thing on this planet going against him? And of course it was late Sunday evening with the emergency dentist closed. The pain was gone now, but he could still feel the exposed root.

28

"So what do you want me to do?"

Tom's voice sounded thin and insecure over the phone.

Sarah had spent all Sunday with Denise discussing her worries about Martin. She knew that his calamitous mood was linked to the negative news from the investors and the many months of overwork, but she was shocked to see him plunge into such dire straits. She had seen it coming gradually, but had never expected that things would deteriorate this fast. The event had somehow triggered a pernicious spot in Martin. Just as a tripwire in a hidden cage, touched in a moment of carelessness, sets in motion a chain reaction of frightening and unforeseen consequences. Like the hateful message he had left her on her mobile. This was not the Martin she knew. It all looked as though nothing could be done, but then, the following day, she had thought of Tom.

"I don't know. Take him somewhere … just take him far away from that flat. He will go mad in there." Sarah spoke quickly, clearly upset by the whole situation.

"I'm not sure–"

"Listen Tom. He's not talking to me and not even to his own family. I've tried everything. He refuses to see a psychologist. I don't think he's talking to anyone. Has he called you?"

"No."

"There, you see. Tom, please. You're the only person who can help him."

Tom was slightly uncomfortable with the new responsibility he was about to be assigned. But Martin was his best and oldest friend – he had to act. Something had to be done quickly before Martin suffocated in his collapsing igloo.

"But what if he says no?"

"I don't know." Sarah began to weep. "Please ... just try." She struggled to pull herself together. "Do it ... for him."

There was a brief silence on the line.

"I'll do everything I can. Sarah, you know you can count on me. Any idea what's going on?"

"I don't know," she sniffed. "It's like he's falling apart. Some weeks ago, he even thought that people were sabotaging the laboratory and spying on him. I ... can't ... I can't stand it Tom ... I'm so worried ... about his health."

"Jesus. And you think he'll listen to me?"

"I don't know. But he'll probably be more open with you than he is with me right now."

Tom heard her blow her nose.

"Please get him out of there," Sarah pleaded. "Just don't tell him I phoned you."

Tom ran through several scenarios that afternoon. Finding a place to go with Martin would be easy. The tough part was to get him lured out of his bed-sit. Once that was pulled off, he was certain Martin could be guided towards other thoughts.

Tom made several attempts to get through to Martin, but in vain. And the inactivated answering machine was indeed very odd. He wondered if Martin had just pulled out all the plugs; so he gave it one last try at nine in the evening, letting the phone ring as long as it could.

Martin finally picked it up.

"Leave me alone, Tom … I'll be okay. I've taken one week off to rest a bit."

"Don't give me that nonsense, Martin. There is no way I will let you go to the dogs."

"Oh, so now I'm going to the dogs … good to know. Who's telling you stupid things like that?"

Tom did his smoothest talking for a long time, but nothing seemed to cheer Martin up or stir up any interest. He did, eventually, agree to Tom taking him to and fetching him from the dentist the following morning, apparently relieved at not having to drive. Tom took Martin's loss of interest in driving as a very serious symptom.

A plan was slowly materializing in Tom's mind. Once he had Martin in the car, he would carry out a full-blown daylight abduction of his best friend and take him to a place he knew would please him. On paper, it sounded simple, but he expected it to be anything but a foregone conclusion.

The next morning, while Martin was sitting in the dentist's chair, full of self-pity and anaesthetics, Tom set up camp in the waiting room, carefully reading an article on the Miss Switzerland election in *Illustré*, all the time keeping an eye on any female patients who happened to pass by.

As the assistant prepared a temporary filling, soon to be replaced by a permanent one, Martin had this strange feeling of being set free from tension and anxiety. For a few moments, a stranger, completely unaware of his personal situation, was taking care of him and there was nothing he could do right now other than let the dentist do her job. Her soft soothing voice was so comforting. He did not have to talk or to do anything. Apart from keeping his mouth wide open, no one expected anything from him right now. He could just lie there – and do nothing. He fell asleep for a few minutes while the dentist was out of the room. He could have slept the whole day in that chair. A whole week. She woke him up with a warm laugh. Who would have thought so? Having a wonderful moment in a dentist's chair.

"Please take me home, Tom," Martin said as he came back, his voice slurred from the anaesthetics in his left jaw.

Tom did not answer; he simply followed Martin out on to the parking lot. They got into Tom's Alfa Romeo and after leaving the car park, Tom headed towards the motorway.

"Where are you going?" Martin said with a deep frown.

"You'll see."

"The hell I will," he yelled. "Just take me home, now!"

"You sound so incredibly funny when *dou dalk dlike dhat*." Tom said, mimicking Martin's unclear pronunciation.

"Tom. Take me home. Now!"

"No!"

Tom did not look at him.

They had just crossed a traffic light when Martin, in a frantic movement of despair, reached down between the front seats and pulled the handbrake with all the force his left arm could mobilize.

The car skidded to a halt on the road. Luckily, no other cars were following them.

Tom held on to the steering wheel with his eyes closed.

"What the HELL are you doing?!"

"Listen, Tom. I'm dead serious now. I'm not going to some bloody loony clinic with you. I am going home." Martin made a movement for the door handle, but before he could manage to swing the door open, Tom stamped on the accelerator and the door slammed shut.

The car leapt forward.

"Now *you* fucking listen!" Tom shouted through the howling sound of the engine while he swiftly changed gears. "You touch that thing again and ... this supposed friend of yours is personally going to beat you up." He steered the car into the slip road leading to the motorway at high speed.

Martin fell silent.

"Don't worry." Tom said. "We're going to spend a little time together. How does that sound?"

Martin looked out of the window, his face reddened with irritation. A muscle around his jaw was making small twitches. He did not answer. They passed through several hill tunnels along the lake and the traffic gradually became smoother. Just before Montreux, beams of sunshine penetrated the thick ceiling of clouds, forming silver spots on the lake, leaving the rest of the water in grey and blue tones.

Tom broke the renewed silence.

"Want to hear a joke?"

"You could have asked me," Martin said with a reproachful expression on his face. "Where are we going?"

"You know that old group *Frankie Goes to Hollywood*"

"How about my clothes? What am I supposed to wear?"

"They've just got back together."

"Sure …"

"In Germany."

"Forgot how they sound."

"They renamed the band *Günther Geht nach Frankfurt.*"

"Great one. My shorts are full."

Tom laughed and shook his head.

"Good start Martin. Let it go, man." He looked towards the mountains. "Let the gloom go."

They passed the end of the lake and entered the valley, which narrowed as they drove, mountain peaks rising high on both sides of the motorway. A sign welcomed them to the *canton* of Valais. Tom pushed on the accelerator.

"Goodbye police canton, hello laid-back canton," he said cheerfully.

Martin cleared his throat and looked at Tom.

"Okay … I'll play along. I'll give it a try. But I don't like surprises, you know that. Where are we going?"

"We're not going to Verbier and we're not going to your parents' place."

"I feel enlightened."

"That's my man! Packed some of my warm gear for you. I know you're not XXL, but don't worry – you won't be posing for a Ralph Lauren show."

"Warm?"

"Yep. We're going to Evolene."

A faint smile of remembrance appeared on Martin's face.

Then it was gone.

29

Menarti had been staying at the Swan clinic for a little over six weeks and seemed to be heading for a remission of his cancer. The pain in his abdomen and the massive skin rashes caused by the therapy had subsided. He could walk without crutches now and some of his appetite had returned.

Lying in bed, he was watching a documentary on television about an Indian tribe in British Columbia in which the elders played an important role for the general well-being of the tribe. When life became predictable, experience would no longer matter to human beings, they said. And so the tribe would relocate every thirty years, to a new place with new streams and new game trails to be figured out.

What a waste of energy, Menarti thought.

His close call with death during the past months had certainly been unpredictable. The fragile tissue of life, at times so loosely woven. All that stuff about people changing their lives after near-death experiences. Why? If someone is happy with his life, has everything he wants without the need to strive for more, when he loves his family and his work, why change it?

Through the open windows, he could hear the sound of crunching gravel coming from the parking ground in front of the clinic. Before getting up, he knew instinctively who it was: Emile Broccaz, the man who had made it all possible. Despite the hefty sum of money he had paid for the treatment, he still owed everything to that man.

Emile Broccaz had one thing to do before seeing Mr Menarti. He entered the main building, briefly greeted one of the nurses who was preparing a tray of food, and headed down the stairs to the basement. He walked through one of the long dimly-lit concrete tunnels and eventually arrived at a metal door, which he unlocked. Behind it was the entrance to another room, with a thick concrete door that had a dark rectangular box on the wall next to it.

A gentle voice asked him to position his head within the face-reader frame markings. He did as requested and a red stroboscope beam swept over his face for a few seconds.

The heavy door slid slowly to one side.

He turned on the lights and a rare smile came to his lips.

This was how a laboratory of the twenty-first century was supposed to look like. Two hundred square meters of heaven, built inside an anti-atomic shelter. Not a single human being – or animal for that sake. Just robots, chemicals and computers. Always searching and testing, generating new knowledge, twenty-four hours a day. A sanctuary for great experiments.

Emile Broccaz looked around and could not help feeling proud of himself. What an achievement! He could live in this place. This was all he needed to be happy. He had actually stayed here for a week, sleeping on a mattress when they installed the computer. It was his brainchild. Beautiful, as it stood there in eight different parts with its many cooling ribs in dark frosty metal, taking up most of the space in the control office, and generating a considerable amount of heat when all the processors were working in parallel.

He switched on a monitor and tapped in three different passwords. There were lots of data in Menarti's file and he read through some of the test results from the three courses of therapy. In the last course they had added an interesting new molecule to the cocktail. It was a protein drug, which Broccaz had procured from the Attis lab freezer. The result had been a complete eradication of Menarti's metastases and no more detectable levels of pancreatic cancer. It was a result beyond all expectations.

How exactly this could happen, Broccaz did not know. They would find out more in the next few months. A second pancreatic cancer patient was on his way.

30

An hour and a half after leaving Lausanne, Tom and Martin arrived in Evolene, a small village nestling in the Hérens valley above Sion. On the left side of the cantonal road, towards the east, a dark, almost brutally-vertical mountain wall rose high above the village. The view to the other side of the village was more welcoming, with smooth rolling hills leading up to snow-sprinkled mountain ranges, offering pleasantly cold hillside air in abundance.

The main street of Evolene was full of old chalets that housed a number of small street-level shops and restaurants. Despite the late autumn weather, the first floor balconies were still full of brightly-coloured flowers and, under the roofs, scores of tiny windows stretched towards the light, which could be very scant in winter. Old converted wooden barns, many delicately perching on a few round straddle stones, were smugly defying the laws of architecture.

Tom skilfully manoeuvred the Alfa along the narrow one-way street through the town centre. The main street was not built for the many cars that were parked along it nowadays. Towards the end of the village, he turned right and parked the car in front of their final destination: an old chalet that had been in Tom's family for three generations.

Minutes later they entered the chalet and walked up the loudly-squeaking stairs to the first floor with the two duffel bags Tom had prepared. The bedrooms were tiny; Martin took the one facing south. It was sparsely equipped with a single bed, a small table and a chair. Nothing had changed in those many years. Even the wood had that same particular, pleasant smell.

Tom had organized the clothing for the first item on Martin's recovery programme, a walk in the hills nearby. Martin opened the duffel bag, and put on Tom's voluminous black fleece sweater and a pair of hiking boots that needed two pairs of socks before they fitted him; he could sense his pulse throbbing in his eardrums. Was it the thin air or something else? He was suddenly drained of energy, too exhausted to move. How he wished he could be elsewhere, in a bed under a warm blanket. Martin lay down on the bed and tried to calm down. What do you call someone who feels both exhausted and agitated at the same time? Confused? Dissociated? Maybe there was no word for it. And if there was no word for it, perhaps no remedy either. What if this contradictory feeling went on forever?

Tom came into the bedroom.

"Everything ready?"

Martin rose slowly from the bed. "Tom. I … I really need a nap before we walk." He knew only too well that he would not be able to relax enough to sleep.

"Wow! You really look sharp with my stuff on!" Tom said, ignoring Martin's remark.

"Tom, listen please! I'm really tired."

"No way! It's not even midday yet! You can sleep later this afternoon when you've had some fresh air."

Tom opened the interior of a backpack filled with sandwiches and water. *"Look! Birdy nam-nam."*

"Please …"

Tom shook his head. "Discussion over. And give me your mobile phone and watch. You don't need them up here."

Martin knew that any further resistance would be utterly in vain. Tom would, if he had to, carry Martin up and down the mountain to achieve his objective. Fighting Tom would be much tougher than just going on the walk. Martin caved in and, dressed in Tom's loose-hanging clothes, followed bravely.

Together they headed off towards La Tour along a path next to the river. At La Tour, Tom took a trail that climbed upwards, heading for the Palanche de la Cretta. The day was quite cloudy but dry and further up the trail they could see how the top of La Dent Blanche shone beautifully when the occasional sunbeam hit it.

Martin said nothing. His feeling of disconnection from the world was worsening. Instead of soft and peaceful mountain slopes, speckled with the red, yellow and green of the pine trees, he was in a world of nothingness. His eyes looked at the small streams they crossed, gently trickling with crystal-clear water, but he could not see the beauty in them. They were just empty images. Unrelated.

Tom did what he could to break the silence. The topics stretched from more or less anything that crossed his mind to his latest insights on the physiology and psychology of women.

Martin tried to listen, but it was difficult. The throbbing pulse in his ears was much better at catching his attention. What was he doing here anyway? Tom's childish and totally ridiculous abduction game was getting on his nerves.

They came to a small hill and Tom ran up to the top. Martin recognized it. He had been here before when they were teenagers.

With a triumphant smile, Tom said, "Remember that amazing ski suit you had on? Man! That thing was so outdated that it was close to becoming fashionable again."

Martin could not laugh. Tom was just not funny. It was as simple as that. Strange that he had never realized it before. How could he ever have thought Tom was funny?

The throbbing pulsations had moved to his throat and upper chest. New thoughts were coming faster now. With each beat.

He wondered what Sarah was up to. Probably enjoying her freedom. He was trapped in this stupid place in the middle of nowhere. All those loose ends. Somebody had to tie them up. Find out what to do with Attis. And their patents? Who would maintain them? Was the centrifuge sabotaged? What was Broccaz up to right now? The bank account, was there any money left? And a new appointment with the dentist. It was all too much to think about.

All of a sudden, Martin's heart jumped a beat. With horror, he realized that his new medication had been forgotten in the hijacking operation. He had none of the pills that had made him feel a little better for the past week. The effects of this morning's capsule were starting to wear off. Fear started to overwhelm him.

"Hey Martin. You have that serious *thinking* look on your face again." Tom took off the backpack and pulled out some sandwiches. "You're thinking too much. Try to relax. Here – take one."

Don't think all the time. Martin's brain was a gang of wild electrons on the loose. He did not control them any longer – they just did whatever they wanted. What was that expression? *Losing your marbles.*

"I really could do with a drink," was the only thing he managed to say.

"Not a bad idea." Tom fetched something from the inner pocket of the backpack. With a grin, he pulled out a silver hip flask and unscrewed the top. "It'd better have something in it ..." he said with a twinkle in his eye.

Martin took a big sip of the whisky and felt the liquid curling downwards through the emptiness, warming it up, giving him some relief for a brief moment. He took a deep breath and said, his voice flat, "What's the plan for tonight?"

"We have a table at *Chez Bernadette,*" Tom said. "And guaranteed free entertainment!"

They came down from the mountains later in the afternoon. Martin tried in vain to take a nap, worrying about how he would ever get through the evening and night. His restlessness became so unbearable that he persuaded Tom to go for some early drinks before dinner.

Chez Bernadette was, according to Tom, second to none for anyone who wanted to unwind. A small, unpretentious wood-built restaurant with a bar, a fireplace for making *raclette* and half a dozen long tables where people would mingle when eating, as in many other alpine cabins. A joist under the ceiling carried the carved names of the main family members. The small windows had red and white chequered curtains. Nothing extraordinary at first sight.

Except Bernadette.

A woman in her late forties, Bernadette often dressed in one of the local traditional costumes. A long black dress and an apron in many bright colours. A band of violet velvet made its way around her waist, which was not among the slimmest in town. Beneath it, she wore a white shirt with short sleeves and a red silk scarf even though, with the fire going, the restaurant was far too hot for that.

Her outgoing personality and her deep, almost provocative, gaze would strike any newcomer in the restaurant. She would meet your eyes, and hold them gently in hers until she had finished looking at your innermost soul. She did it in a way that was quite pleasant, with sincere interest and well-meant purpose.

The air was almost free of smoke and melted cheese when Tom and Martin arrived. That would all change in a couple of hours.

Bernadette appeared from the kitchen.

"Bonjour ma jeunesse!"

She immediately pointed out to the four locals at the bar and the other waitress how handsome the two new male visitors were. Tom and Martin were greeted with friendly laughs.

"Tell me, how's the family?" Bernadette said, holding Tom's arm.

"They're fine. We're all coming up for Christmas."

"Good."

Her long dark hair was pinned up with just a few wisps dangling loosely. She studied Martin for a brief moment with a tender smile and strong grey-blue eyes. "Come and sit over here, my two little sweethearts."

She motioned them to the end of a long table close to the bar and Tom ordered a jug of *Fendant*, a white wine from the region.

The men at the bar were of various ages and they spoke loudly in *patois*, a local dialect. They were in their working clothes, several of them with faces tanned as dark as the lacquered wooden panels on the walls, and were drinking white wine from small tumblers. There was not much space in the restaurant so Bernadette had to push by them a little every time she went out into the kitchen.

One of them, a stout man named Jean with a barrel-shaped torso, spoke with a voice that indicated his ready participation in the growth of the cigarette industry. His blue trousers had spots of dirt and he wore a yellow cap. Next to him stood a lad in his early twenties, the quietest of the group, with fluorescent orange trousers and a thick brown chequered shirt.

"Don't pretend to be drinking!" Jean said to his younger neighbour.

"I was just thinking."

"You can't do that!"

"What do you mean?"

"Drink ... or don't drink. But do something!"

" ... "

One of the other men intervened. He was in his mid-fifties and had a lined face. His curry-yellow knitted cardigan was wide open. He spoke very loudly. "Jean. You always WAFFLE!

That poor young lad is all confused now, you crazy peasant. The problem with you Jean is that you talk far too much shit!!"

"If you can't say anything stupid in this bar, then where the hell can you?" Jean said.

"Go talk to your cows. Look at you! Hundred watts in the belly – no light in the bulb."

Bernadette came by.

"No loud philosophizing, PLEASE! We've got other guests." She looked firmly at them all. "Okay … anything more to drink, gentlemen?"

"Yes, but no alcohol for me … I'll just have some wine," the man in the red fleece said.

Laughter all through the bar.

Tom was listening to their conversation. He started small-talking with them.

Martin's mind was controlled by other elements and he remained sombre as he kept forcing it to stay within the four walls. Whatever he tried, he just could not focus on the current moment. *Those pills*. If only he had just one, right now. His throat went dry and he felt anxiety creeping back inside him.

Bernadette came with the white wine and filled up their glasses. Martin drank the entire glass in one go.

"He doesn't talk much, your friend," the man in the yellow cardigan said, looking at Tom.

"My friend has an important problem to solve," Tom said. "He's a scientist. Sometimes needs a lot of deep thinking." He made the index finger move in demonstrative circles around his temple.

"The next Einstein perhaps?" One of the other sun-tanned men emptied his small glass of white wine. "I could see that something was wrong. But then again, that's how scientists are."

"I know what science is about," the man in the red fleece said, eagerly puffing on his pipe. "It's like when you trepan a mosquito."

"… trepan?"

"Yes. You drill a whole through its brain to take away its urge to sting. Expensive as hell for that kind of result, but that's research for you … in a nutshell."

"Shut up, you idiot." One of the other men pretended to give him a slap on the head.

"One should never drink on an empty brain," Tom said with amusement.

The men in the bar howled with laughter.

"That's a good one. I'll remember that one," the man in the yellow cardigan said.

"Hey!" One of the other men gestured vividly. "We've run out of wine. What's happening?"

The barman was on the way in through the front door, carrying a pile of wood for the fireplace.

"That wine's coming really slowly, mister! You have haemorrhoids or something?"

"Just a minute. I'll check with the kitchen."

Tom laughed loudly and turned towards Martin. "Christ! What a bunch of characters."

Bernadette brought the first two portions of *raclette*. Tom ground a handsome amount of pepper all over the melted cheese, potatoes and pickles – then emptied the plate in three mouthfuls. Martin slowly ate some of the cheese and the pickle. His hunger was disturbed by a strange fluttering in his chest and a pounding sensation in his neck. Sweat broke out on his forehead. Even without the pullover, it was really hot in here. He tried to breathe more deeply and took another massive gulp of white wine, hoping this would help. It had in the afternoon.

Bernadette came by their table and Tom ordered a second portion. Martin declined.

"He's not eating, your friend. What's wrong? *Chagrin d'amour?*"

"Just general chagrin," Tom said.

"My poor little olive tree. Your roots all dried out?"

She bent down and put an arm around Martin's shoulder.

"I'll make a special portion for you. You'll see. It'll help." She stood up and wiggled back between the crowded tables towards the kitchen.

People, smoke and the smell of melted cheese progressively filled up the room as the evening unfolded. Tom got increasingly inebriated and spoke mostly with the locals. Martin's gaze had several times gone on infinite, prompting Tom to ask what he could do to bring him on other thoughts. Martin said simply that he was OK and then Tom fired off another joke, which each time landed successfully in the bar.

The wine gave Martin some relief but also a growing headache. The world was passing by, not like a film, but like a sequence of snapshots. Random patterns in a kaleidoscope without colours. Haphazardly. From the outside, his face remained almost expressionless. Inside he felt like twisted steel.

At the sixth portion of *raclette*, Tom lost his patience.

"Come on! Don't be so glum!"

"I'm not," Martin snapped "I'm just leaving all the nonsense talk to you."

Tom jumped.

"Oh! Great! Thanks a million. So that's the way you thank your best friend? For organizing this?"

"I'm just getting tired of hearing your old jokes over and over again. That's all." Martin immediately regretted what he had said.

That was a severe body blow to Tom. Few men had ever told him he was not funny. He was fuming. "If you weren't my best friend and in that shitty state, I'd ask you to step outside."

"I'm sorry. I … I'm not quite myself today."

Tom's generous mood could flip around with the wrong remark and it often changed at some point when he was getting drunk.

Like an exhausted child going over the top, his humour would become increasingly nasty. From past experience, Martin knew that there was a moment where things could get out of hand. That moment was very close now. It was time to leave.

"Right."

"Let's go home."

"I need a last one." Tom looked exhausted. "Bernadette! A *pression* and the bill, please."

She came over with the beer and the bill and went over to clear some plates away from another table. As Tom pulled out his wallet, half a dozen coins dropped to the ground, rolling across the floor.

Two of the locals were still in the bar. One of them picked up a coin and said, jokingly, "Sure you've got enough money in that wallet? … to throw it around like that?"

He laughed at his own joke.

"You know what?" Tom said as he, slightly staggering, turned his large menacing frame towards the man, who took a step backwards.

"No?"

"Sure you've got enough teeth in that mouth? … to talk like that?"

"Let's go now." Martin pulled Tom's sleeve.

"In a minute," Tom said still looking at the man in the bar.

"IT'S TIME!" Bernadette's mighty voice cut straight across the room.

"Yes. You're right." Tom turned round.

Martin had already gone.

31

Physically exhausted by his afternoon hike and the worse for wear after the boozy evening *Chez Bernadette*, Martin fell asleep immediately in his bed in the tiny, wood-panelled bedroom of Tom's family chalet.

Just two hours into his deep, dreamless sleep, Martin woke up, covered in sweat, his head throbbing. The walls and ceiling were engulfing him in terrifying feelings of claustrophobia. The air was thick, too thick to enter his mouth or nose, and he gasped for breath.

Lost in the dark, he jumped up and ran forward. He came up against a wood-panelled wall, making a loud thump that reverberated throughout the chalet. The only sound that followed was Tom's unrelenting comatose snoring in the next room. Martin felt no pain, only more panic. He had to get out at once, but where was the door, where was the handle?

He searched feverishly in the darkness. His heart was pounding faster and faster, his whole body thumping like timpani. He came close to screaming for help, when his hands finally found the door-frame.

Once outside the chalet, he filled his lungs with the cold, still air. Heavy snowflakes fell from the dark sky on to his naked feet. He could feel in his throat the excruciatingly sour taste of heartburn, a reminder of all the white wine he had drunk.

He had no idea what time it was. With the best of intentions, Tom had hidden his watch somewhere safe, and his mobile phone was probably in that same hideout as well.

More than anything else Martin wanted to go home, but both he and Tom were in no state to drive a car right now. The only solution would be a bus in the early morning. That meant waiting several hours. Shivers ran through Martin's legs as he went back inside.

The couch in the living room was not at all comfortable – but there was no way he could go back to sleep in that tiny bedroom. After he lay down, his body started its strange and uncontrollable behaviour again, his heart beating its way up to his throat, cold sweat running down his neck.

What was his body doing to him?

Martin clenched his teeth.

I have to keep myself straight.

For another two gruelling sleepless hours, he waited for the first glimmers of daylight to appear, wondering if he would ever be able to sleep normally again. He needed that anti-anxiety pill so badly that he could have screamed in self-pity.

The first bus to Sion would leave at a quarter to six. Martin stood at the bus stop, freezing, waiting for it to come. He had searched in vain for both his watch and mobile phone. At least he had his keys and wallet – that was all he needed right now.

There was no way he could have woken up Tom. Martin remembered insulting him the night before. *'I'm just getting tired of hearing your old jokes'.* Why had he said that? To make Tom feel the pain he himself was feeling? Tom was just trying to lead his best friend on to different thoughts – yet Martin had punished him for it. Why?

Once in Sion, Martin boarded a train and an hour later, he took a taxi home from Lausanne station. Although he felt dead tired, he had not been able to sleep on the train. His legs almost collapsed beneath him as he climbed up to the fourth floor.

Back in the flat, he locked the door with only one thing in mind: get the toilet bag in the bathroom, the one that contained the blister pack with the elixir he had been yearning for.

He washed the pill down with a full glass of water, shocked by his reflection in the mirror. He could not believe what he saw. Was that really the face of the young, promising entrepreneur who had once created one of the most exciting start-ups in Lausanne?

Couldn't be. That thing in the mirror looked more like a ghost than anything else.

He felt like one. How could anyone be dead tired and fired up on all cylinders – at the same time?

What was happening to him?

I'm not behaving like myself, I don't look like myself.

Why wasn't the damn pill working yet? He had taken these pills for over a week now and the effect always kicked in quickly. Martin wondered if the drug was losing its effect and feverishly pulled out another pill from the blister pack, swallowing it with a quick gulp of water.

He looked at his own image in the mirror again.

Those bloody venture capitalists had started it all. Dragging him round in circles. Like cats, or rather, fat cats, playing with a freshly-caught mouse. Not particularly interested in eating, just keeping themselves entertained.

Martin pulled out a strand of grey hair.

No, he had to stop blaming the VCs. There were just too many people suffering from chronic 'victimitis' who preferred to complain all the time. Something could be done about the situation.

While he looked at the strand of hair, he suddenly became aware of a slight blurring of vision. He blinked his eyes several times and tried to focus harder. But the blurring continued and worsened. The hair in his hand was no longer visible.

It was all happening so quickly, like a shutter being pulled over his eyes. Horrified, he could feel his sight gradually starting to fade.

"Jesus! Help!" he heard himself crying aloud.

Completely helpless, he could only stand there passively as the darkness closed in on him.

32

M artin screamed, holding on to the bathroom table.
He rubbed his eyes, opening and closing them frantically;
fumbling around the basin, he eventually found the tap. He bent
down and splashed water all over his face, but to no avail. Even
with his eyes wide open, he could still see nothing. There was no
pain, just total obscurity.

"What's this? What the hell's going on?" He shouted
desperately into his new world of looming darkness.

He continued to rinse his eyes.

Thoughts raced through his head. What could he do?

The front door. *Go down the staircase to the neighbours.*
Somebody had to be at home. Not the ones below, they were
never there during the day, but perhaps those lower down.

With a heart beating wildly, Martin felt his way out of the
bathroom. His insecure hands gripped for the rough-hewn wall
and followed it carefully round the corner. From there, he knew
he could feel his way to the front door. Moving too fast, he
almost stumbled over a chair. Cursing loudly, he wondered how
he could have forgotten the old wooden chair that came from his
grandmother. It had always been there.

What was happening to his eyes?

He found the handle of the front door and pushed it down. The
door was locked. He remembered locking it, but where had he
put the keys?

Please don't panic. Don't panic now, Martin.

Where had he left them? They were not in his trouser pocket. The cupboard!

He turned around to reach for the cupboard he knew stood opposite the front door and ran his hands all over the surface, but there was nothing!

Please, this is not happening. Where are the keys?

He had to hold back his panic. If it took over, he would be lost.

His fingers touched the phone. Yes, that would be the solution. He would call for help. He reached for it too hurriedly and pushed over the small lamp that stood next to it. The bulb shattered as the lamp hit the floor. Thin splinters of glass crushed underneath his shoes as he moved.

His hand finally clasped the phone, pulling it from its cradle. His legs were beginning to tremble. He could hear the dialling tone, but what about the buttons? Were they the same as on his mobile? He could not remember. Who should he call? Emergency? No, Sarah first.

He pushed frantically everywhere on the handset, but all he got were beeps in different tones. He had no idea which buttons he was hitting, his hands were trembling far too much.

Suddenly, a number was being speed-dialled.

Relieved, he heard the phone ringing. He had no idea who he was calling, but it had to be someone either he or Sarah knew.

"Hello," a male voice said. Martin did not recognize it immediately.

"I need help … urgently. Who is this … please?"

"Lorne. Lorne Falcroft."

"Oh … Is your father there?"

"Who's calling?"

"Please! Just let me talk to your father."

"Martin, is that you?"

"Yes."

"You've actually called my mobile. My father is abroad. What's wrong?"

Lorne's mobile. Sarah had called him!

"I ... Jesus ... I've lost my eyesight. I ... I've just gone blind!"

"What happened? Did you have an accident?"

"I need to go to the hospital."

"Are you at home?"

"Yes. Please, get me a taxi quickly."

"I'm just walking distance away from where you live."

"No. Wait!"

"I'll call a doctor for you on my way over." Lorne was panting while he ran with the phone in his hand.

After what seemed like an eternity, Martin could hear the front door being unlocked and someone thanking the landlord for his help.

"Lorne, is that you?" he said from the sofa.

"Yes." Lorne came over and sat down next to him.

Martin was breathing rapidly. He had rubbed his eyes so hard that tears were coming down his cheeks. "I can't see a thing! Christ! What's happening?"

"Leave your eyes alone. Try to relax for a moment."

"RELAX?? Can you even imagine what this feels like?" Martin shrieked. He regretted not making other phone calls. "Get me a doctor right now."

"You'll get one. I promised you. One of the finest ophthalmologists in the region is on her way."

Martin could not understand why it took so long. All the problems he had faced so far suddenly seemed trivial in comparison with this pitch-blackness. Prompted by Lorne, he gave a hasty account, as coherently as he could, of the morning's events – the train journey back from Evolene, his deep anxiety, the pills that didn't seem to work any more and the terrifying moment when he lost his eyesight.

"Neither you nor I know what is going on inside your body right now," Lorne said, "but until the doctor gets here, maybe we could try to understand what your body is telling you."

"For God's sake Lorne, don't give me that peace-love-and-vegetable stuff! This is real life! Did you ever lose *your* sight? What if I stay blind?"

The thought was unbearable. It stressed him out more than anything else. *Why didn't the bloody anxiety medication work?*

"I want a pill. Get me another anti-anxiety pill."

"How many have you taken already?"

"I don't know. A couple. Please. Lorne, they're in the bathroom somewhere."

"Listen. I don't think pills will do you any good right now. Let's wait until the doctor arrives. Who knows, maybe that medication you took played some role in what happened."

Martin was breathing faster.

"So when is that bloody doctor coming? I … just can't take any more of this. It's too much …"

He felt Lorne's hand on his shoulder.

"There is another way," Lorne said calmly. "Give me ten minutes." He spoke with surprising conviction. "Just ten. You've got nothing to lose."

Instinctively Martin wanted to resist. Apart from getting his eyesight back, there was nothing in the world that could make him relax. He hoped that Lorne had been telling the truth when he said he had called a doctor. That was the only thing that mattered right now. He could not believe that he was now forced to put his faith in someone like Lorne. But there really was no choice. He had to endure another ten gruelling minutes.

"Well, then, do whatever you think you can do," Martin murmured.

Lorne suggested that they both sit on the sofa without moving. Martin found the silence slightly uncomfortable. Darkness and silence. He could hear the sound of an ambulance going by on the main street outside, its siren blaring.

"Okay, let's start with you focusing only on your breathing. Try to notice the texture, the softness of your breath and the air you inhale."

As Martin half-heartedly began to breathe under Lorne's guidance, he sensed how his face muscles slowly started to relax, his jaw dropping lower. It felt as if the air had more substance, more oxygen in it.

"For now, just go on listening without judging what I say. Concentrate on your breathing as if it were the only thing you would ever want for the rest of your life. Use your breath to cleanse your body. Breathe out one concern with each exhalation."

Martin closed his eyes and leant back, exhaling one fear after another. There were enough moments of anger and anxiety to make him breathe forever, but he did start to sense some lightness. Like an astronaut in outer space, he was in a state of weightlessness and could feel the peaceful expression on his face, like Sarah's when she was sleeping.

The words came almost independently. They were so clear. Martin was listening.

Lorne's soft, tranquil voice continued. "There is a universal truth, a pool of knowledge, of truthfulness, in which you just know things are right. Like an intelligence beyond the mind. You tap into that pool and it flows with all the right answers. You can't always explain why. You just *know.*"

An infinite new world had started speaking to him. It was such a strange new place. So amazingly calm. The words seemed to flow into him like tiny particles. It was not the meaning of each word that spoke to him, but rather the vibration itself, like pure, uninterpreted energy.

From time to time, Lorne stopped talking and made him listen to the silence. At first, Martin wanted to fill the emptiness by saying something, commenting or arguing, but he could not. The words would not fit in.

Martin had no idea how much time had passed. Maybe two minutes, or fifteen, or maybe even an hour. His sense of time had been outmanoeuvred, and for the first time in his whole life, it did not worry him one little bit. What he cared about was his heart now beating regularly again.

Lorne's voice became firmer.

"Our mind plays some amazing games with us. It's the world's best manipulator and we have been taught to obey it. Our entire upbringing is based on the belief that rational skills are superior to intuition. In most situations in life, that helps us to pull through safely. But what happens when something extraordinary crops up? When we are forced to think outside the box? When our old beliefs are just not good enough? When our body starts disagreeing and, in a desperate cry for help, falls ill?"

Difficult questions. All of them. Martin had not a clue about any possible answers, but he knew that they were getting closer to something essential. Things had changed. A tiny cogwheel amongst thousands of others was getting ready to spin in the opposite direction.

"Do you remember how your company name, Attis Therapeutics, came to you?"

Martin took a deep breath and reflected. The name had been so natural at the time. He had found it by glancing through a list of Greek mythology names. A fertility god. Attis was a great name for the venture. Everyone had loved it.

"Do you remember what happened to him?" Lorne asked.

Martin did, but he had somehow pushed it out of his conscious thinking.

"To satisfy the expectations of two women in love with him," Lorne continued, "Attis was caught up in a spree of self-destruction until he eventually died."

Martin was glad that he could keep his eyes closed. He knew all the details of the story. How Attis, the son of a god and a mortal human being, had cried on the top of Mount Dindymus that he deserved the pain he was going through. How he had mangled his body with a sharp stone and how, in the end, he had bled to death.

"Names never come by coincidence," Lorne said. "We tell ourselves that we pick names out of the blue. But that's not true. Names often fit far better than we would like them to. And they carry a lot of weight for the course of events."

Martin thought of the end of the story. Attis eventually turned into a pine-tree, his self-mutilation, death and resurrection a symbol of the fruits of the earth, dying in winter only to rise again in spring.

"Something deep inside you knew that you would go through a similar experience. Trying to please your beliefs and your heart, both at the same time.

Martin thought of what Gavin had said.

I can give you a good recipe for failure and that is trying to please everybody.

Right now, Lorne was actually saying the same thing. Could it be that Lorne and Gavin, two people whom he had thought were diametrically opposed to each other, were in essence in complete agreement?

"Pleasing our beliefs can be very dangerous for everything we undertake. We build our lives on beliefs that we have taken over from the past and from our environment," Lorne said, "from ancestors, parents, teachers, doctors. Our beliefs are extremely powerful. We even believe that those beliefs are our own and that they represent true reality. They do become reality, but it is only *one* of several possible realities. For example, if you truly believe that everything you do in life is going to be difficult and full of suffering then it will turn out exactly like that – so that your mind is pleased with its game mode."

"A self-fulfilling prophecy," Martin said solemnly.

"It can be avoided," Lorne said. "The first thing is to realize that we've gone astray. That we've been running down the wrong road."

"So simple and obvious," Martin said, with some irony in his tone. "But, practically speaking, just how do we do that?"

"By starting to look carefully at the signposts. All of them. The problem is that we only take them at face value. That's why we get lost. We don't take time to understand the underlying message. Signposts are small at first and grow bigger the further you go down the wrong road. Very far down, they are huge and tend to stand in the middle of the road so you can't avoid crashing into them."

Martin was thinking for a moment.

"And now I've crashed into a big one?"

"What does your body tell you?"

"I hate it when you answer me with more questions."

"Don't they offer interesting answers?"

Martin suddenly felt dizzy. Like when you get up too quickly after sitting or lying down and all the blood rushes from your brain. It was all too big to handle right now. He was back in the darkness, back in scary reality. The panic was galloping back.

"Oh God. All this talk. I still can't see a thing!"

Before Lorne could say anything, the doorbell rang. Lorne went out to open the door. Martin could hear him speaking with a woman, then they both came into the living-room.

33

A t the other end of the lake, in Geneva, an investor conference was taking place. Tanya was in the audience, waiting for the first biotech company presentation to begin. She flicked through the conference catalogue, wondering where Martin was right now. It had been a week since he had taken time off to recover from an apparent burnout. She had not heard from him at all.

On the platform stood a middle-aged CEO who had been introduced as a serial entrepreneur by one of the organizers. The CEO spoke with ease to a hall packed with people.

"… The first time I made a company presentation here was sixteen years ago. It was a pitch for my first start-up, one of those late afternoon presentations. Nobody knew me and there was just one other person in the room. You can probably imagine how upset I was. Only *one* person listening to the presentation I had prepared for *weeks*! So with all the frustration I'm feeling, I walk down to this fellow to thank him personally for coming to my talk. Slightly surprised, he shakes my hand and says: 'Don't thank me, I'm just the next speaker' …"

The audience exploded with laughter.

While the CEO went on with his presentation, Tanya glanced round the room and recognized several of the VCs they had been speaking to in the past. They were all ears, wanting to hear about a company going into its last financing round, fulfilling their dreams about a quick, low-risk return on investment in less than two years with an initial public offering, an IPO, of the company's shares on the stock exchange. A long queue of VCs would be waiting to talk to that CEO afterwards.

In the darkness of the room, a few seats in front of her, Tanya noticed Kohler. From time to time he looked back. At the end of the session, Kohler immediately came towards her and suggested that they have a coffee at the small buffet in the corridor outside the presentation rooms.

"How are things with the company? I'm surprised none of you are presenting."

Tanya explained how Upfront Ventures for some strange reason had backed out just before they were due to sign the final contract.

"We never really found out why."

"I thought everything was signed and set for you," Kohler said with genuine surprise. "What will happen now?"

"I don't know. We'll see. Maybe someone will take out a license on the patents."

Kohler thought for a moment. Tanya could see that some new idea was hatching in his mind.

"Listen. Perhaps we could meet together, all three of us? You, Martin and I."

Tanya wondered how Martin would react to this. The last time she had spoken to him about venture capitalists, he had gone berserk.

Any venture capitalist who comes walking through this door with an unsigned contract will be given a free taste of our hazardous chemical waste container!

She was less emotional about it all, although she too realized that providing free educational seminars for VCs was not the most fulfilling mission in life.

"Listen Tanya. I'm sorry for what happened, but there was little I could do for you at the time. I tried to push for an accelerated approval process, but unfortunately it didn't take off."

"Don't get me wrong," Tanya said. "I'm not against meeting with you. It's just, well, to be quite frank, I have no idea of where Martin has gone. He isn't in great shape. So you see, right now, I just have too many loose ends that need tying up. Both personal and business-wise."

With no further ado, she picked up her shoulder bag, said goodbye to Kohler and left, ever more nervous about how Martin was doing.

34

The concrete-walled computer room underneath the Swan clinic rumbled with the quiet hum of electricity running through the many processors of the supercomputer that stood in the middle of the room.

Emile Broccaz was planning his weekly schedule.

On sleep medication and in apparent remission from his pancreatic cancer, Mr Menarti had been transported back to his family today. The three courses of experimental anti-cancer treatment had succeeded far beyond anyone's expectations. No residual cancer cells could be detected anywhere in Menarti's body.

The surprising discoveries in the clonogenic lab on Menarti's cancer cells were confirmed with striking results. The Attis experimental drug had a highly synergistic effect when used in combination with some of the other anti-cancer compounds.

They had turned a certain death sentence into a cure. The three courses of aggressive therapy had left him weak and it would take months before he got his strength back – but he now had a new lease of life. Broccaz wondered whether Menarti would be smart enough to grasp that opportunity. With the stories he had heard from the nursing staff, he guessed that Menarti would probably start by spending some time with his family, then rapidly get bored and return to his role as the modern working hero. History always repeated itself.

Not that Broccaz really cared. He had received more than he could have hoped for. Another patient, desperate but rich, paying for being a guinea pig in a human trial that had provided invaluable data on a cancer type, which they had never dared to work on before. Broccaz wanted it that way. A clean ending with no more discussions or questions.

His deep involvement with Attis Therapeutics had come at the right moment in time and had paid off handsomely: in record time, he had found a treatment for pancreatic cancer, one of the toughest illnesses to deal with. From this day forward, he was confident that he could cure any form of cancer.

Broccaz was amazed that no one in the Attis laboratory had noticed the fake vial of lyophilized powder, which, one month before, he had placed there instead of the real therapeutic protein. And he was pleased about the well-orchestrated *phishing* attack, the harmless-looking personalized e-mail to the lab technicians, that had opened the gates to a large part of the network of the university from which his data-mining programs could find any information he might want.

All his efforts to slow down the progress of the company, so that it would fit into his elaborate game plan, had been carried out smoothly and accurately.

He was rather proud of how he had been able to orchestrate the ultracentrifuge failure without hurting anyone. The lab clean-up process had gone as expected. After the crash, one of his men had immediately removed residues from the explosives to make sure no detectable traces would be left on the ultracentrifuge. It would just look like rotor blade metal fatigue. Two other men, dressed as electrical repair workers had cleared out the remaining surveillance equipment and software that could not be removed from a remote location. These included various bugging devices, network sniffers, PC keystroke tracking devices. It was easy to install spyware on computers, but a bit more awkward to remove them again. Some of the PC's had passwords but they had managed to crack them all. Using his lab key, the men could go in and out whenever they wanted. With the current state of the lab, no suspicions had been raised at all.

Martin and Tanya had been perfect for the start-up. Two reliable pawns on the grand chessboard. Martin had been a great goalkeeper, firmly holding on to his belief that lack of money was the main root of his misery. This aspect of human beings was what Broccaz liked the most. The naïve illusion that they were thinking freely when, in fact, they could be manipulated to do almost anything once you fully understood the life patterns they lived by. That made business a lot easier for him.

A growing problem, however, was Martin's recent erratic behaviour. Broccaz had always thought of him as a relatively stable and resourceful person and was somewhat surprised by his rapid slide into something that looked like a full-blown depression. All the symptoms were there. Developing paranoia was one of them.

Broccaz did not like loose ends, and this indeed was one. It could turn into a problem. He swung his office chair towards a keyboard, entered a couple of passwords and watched the map on the screen. The little triangle of Martin's mobile phone tracer was still blinking on the electronic map near Evolene; the phone was on, but he could not hear any sounds. What was Martin doing out there?

He did not like that at all. Unusual things had begun to happen in the past few days. Events that did not add up. The time had come for him to pull the plug on Attis and toss all the babies out with the bathwater.

35

Gabriella, the ophthalmologist, a woman in her late fifties, was a good friend of Lorne's. She examined Martin's eyes as he sat on the sofa. Deep in concentration, she inspected Martin's pupils and irises with a small lamp, illuminating them from different angles. She pulled down each of his lower eyelids to study the white sclera, all the while asking him questions about his general state of health. Being with her had some of the same soothing effect as when he had been at the dentist with his chipped tooth. Nobody was asking anything else of him except to relax.

Martin told her about the stress that had dramatically worsened in the previous months, about his sleeping problems and the weight he had put on. Her continued questioning led them to speak about his anxieties and the medication he so rapidly was becoming dependent on.

"Somehow I have become … how shall I put it … trapped?" he said.

Gabriella sat back.

"I can't tell exactly what the underlying cause of your sudden blindness is. There could be many. It could be both psychological and physiological. But when it happens suddenly like this, chances are good that we can revert your vision back to normal again."

She spoke in such a gentle voice. Martin thought he could perceive her small silhouette in the darkness.

"All the same, I would like to examine you at the hospital." She looked at her watch. "It's almost ten now. It would have to be round about midday."

Lorne stood up. "While you two finish, I'll go clean up the glass from the floor in the entrance, so no one cuts their feet."

Even though it annoyed him that Lorne was there to witness his misery, Martin could not help feeling amazed about his unexpected drive and determination and was grateful that he had come by so quickly. He had misjudged Lorne's personal qualities; there was definitely a bit of Gavin in him. Just expressed very differently.

Gabriella gave Martin a simple blood thinner and told him to rest for the next two hours. Then Lorne could bring him to the hospital.

After the ophthalmologist left and Lorne had helped him into bed, Martin wondered what would happen if she turned out to be wrong, if he stayed blind and became dependent on other people. That was an unbearable thought.

The difference between blind and deaf people. Yes, now he remembered. *Blind people are disconnected from things and deaf people are disconnected from other people.*

So why was it scarier to become blind?

Because the world relied on *things*?

In the still of the bedroom, he wondered why he was not panicking.

I should be but I'm not.

Whatever way you looked at it, his life was in shambles. He had reached absolute nadir, an all-time low, with his blindness overshadowing everything else.

So, again, why did he feel so calm?

No logic could explain this calmness. He did not trust it. Was it just another illusion? Another fleeting part of his life that made less and less sense? He wondered what was going on in there, in his mind, deeply buried in the unexplained darkness.

An image of his father appeared in his mind. The weather-beaten body. He remembered a phrase his father had used so often. A mantra for his family, always living hand-to-mouth. *Never trust the moment when you stop having difficulties. It's a short-lived delusion from the world of the lazy man.*

Pictures drifted gently through the inescapable liquid of his visionless eyes. The busy family winery during the autumn school holidays. The wine cellars with their smell of humid, mouldy dust. His two sisters running in the sun-drenched vineyards, the warm air flowing upwards with the earthy smell mixing with the scents of sweet ripe grapes. The straight lines of reddening leaves and green-yellow berries. The colours in deep mysterious shades. The intoxicating fruity fumes. He could smell them all.

At certain periods, the whole family had to work hard, not only in the vineyards, but also in the adjacent apricot orchards to supplement their income, from early morning until evening. Even in winter Martin's dad was always busy doing something, repairing vehicles and buildings, never asking for help from anybody other than members of the family and never paying a salary. Despite that, they never had enough to live on. Some of the other wine growers were better at making money and worked less hard. Martin never understood how that could be. Dad's finances always were in an 'incomprehensible mess' as his mother used to put it. Making money was complicated. Conversations around the dinner table were about saving money, not about creating more of it. It was all about scrimping and saving. The same frustrating message all the time: 'Be restrictive in your life until you die. Save yourself to death.'

He had wanted to break free from all that; the world of science had been his refuge. A conscious choice of a field far removed from the world in which he had grown up.

'All this highfalutin science!' his father always said. 'Makes your head spin without getting you anywhere. You deserve better than that, son. And who's going to keep this place going?' Then his father would put on that sulky look Martin had come to hate so much.

Had he escaped one cage, only to find himself imprisoned in another? Or was it just another room in the same cage? He could not tell what was shutting him in, but he knew it was there. How long did this have to go on? Everything had gone wrong lately. Would a time ever come when things started to go right?

Serendipity.

The powerful yet treacherous word he had heard pronounced for the first time by a professor at the University of Southern California. Half-way between knowing and not knowing what you were searching for. Tom's version of serendipity was looking for a needle in a haystack and then finding a farmer's beautiful daughter in there. Somehow, it was linked to coincidences and luck – or the lack of it.

Had he ever been a scientist? Perhaps he was searching too hard, unable to lose himself in the process. Not a winegrower, not a scientist, not a CEO. Not capable of keeping a wonderful girl like Sarah. So of what use was he to the world?

He felt he was swimming in a black lake, not knowing how deep or how wide it was, unable to distinguish between up and down, sky and surface, wondering all the time how much longer he would have to swim in it. If he reached the shore, would it be steep and slippery, preventing him from climbing out of the darkness? And what was awaiting him outside?

Just when life began to seem meaningful and bright and everything appeared to be on track, why was it that meaninglessness kicked in again and just blew the whole thing right up in his face?

All that effort. To what purpose?

If he had to remain blind, so be it! He didn't want to fight any more. He was so tired of it. Other people could do the fighting; there were more than enough of them.

His eyes suddenly started to feel as heavy as bricks and his mind began clicking on and off. His whole body argued listlessly that nothing he could conquer right now would be as desirable as sleep. He tried to resist for a little while, but sensed his mind and body letting go, then dozed off.

36

The wind and the change in temperature had turned the snow into ice. Martin was sledging with two friends on a long, steep slope in the hills high up above his family's farm. He was nine years old and screaming with joy. The boys were making their game into a race. Far in front of the others, speeding along all too fast, Martin lost control of his sledge and found himself unable to slow down.

Now he was dreaming about it all over again.

The shouting. His own screams. The barbed wire cutting the lower left side of his chin. The taste of blood and metal inside his mouth. The red snow. The scars that would never fully disappear.

In his fitful slumber, the events triggered chain reactions in his mind, with each conscious experience as an epicentre. Ripples were travelling all across his brain, recruiting more neurons on the way, ending in avalanches of fear.

Martin woke up with a jump that made him fall out of bed.

"You all right?" Lorne asked, holding his arm to help him up again. "Hope you didn't hurt yourself. You were screaming in your sleep."

Only half-awake, Martin's head was still seething with activity from the vivid dream and from the impact with the floor. He took a few moments to gather himself together, sitting on the bed with his back against the wall. His sight had still not come back.

He told Lorne about the dream. It was one of the few childhood memories where all the details had remained with him ever since.

"I couldn't stop the sledge, Lorne. No matter what I tried. I let go and had a horrible accident."

"Don't you find that interesting?" Lorne asked. "I mean, dreaming about that event right now?"

Martin did not know what to say.

"But you're wrong about one important detail, Martin. You didn't let go. You lost control."

Lorne fell silent for a moment.

"There's a big difference between losing control and letting go. Your body knows it. Fear follows on from loss of control. Peace follows on from letting go."

Without moving from where he was sitting at the foot of the bed, Lorne asked: "Can you think of a situation where you did let go? Where you fully trusted someone else to help you reach your goal?"

At that same instant, the image of a narrow path on a mountain rim came into Martin's mind. He was on a trek with Sarah, accompanied by two guides, making the final climb from the Barafu camp to the Uhuru summit at almost six thousand metres altitude on the Kilimanjaro. The porters who carried food, tents and clothes had all stayed behind at the camp.

He never had any doubts about the two young guides leading the way through the magic star-lit night. They knew the way. All he had to do was to pay attention to the path and take care of his body walking on it. Nothing else. Second by second, he remained on the alert, listening to what his body was telling him. Was he panting too much? Was the small headache above his left ear growing worse? Was he thirsty? Would his stamina last all the way to the top?

He would never forget the feeling when he and Sarah reached the summit after a last gruelling hour of climbing. At that moment, nothing else in the world mattered. All the pain had gone and the sun was rising. And with it came a sense of sheer relief and happiness.

"Try to stay in that feeling of letting go," Lorne said, "and of being fully in the present."

It was quiet in the bedroom and Martin noticed the regularity of his own breath.

"It's possible to let go in any situation," Lorne continued. "And not just on the Kilimanjaro, but in everyday life, there are guides to lead you, Martin. They appear in the form of people and situations that sometimes may seem negative to you and which you perceive as a menace."

"I'm not sure I follow you ..."

"Okay, remember the signposts we spoke about? Guides, messages, signposts – they are really part of the same universal effort to help you in your experience. The problem is that we desperately cling to the obvious. But just like an iceberg, most of the important matter is out of sight. When we deny the existence of the invisible world, we deprive ourselves of the most valuable dimension in our life experience: the magic."

Martin scratched his chin, then turned his head upwards. Listening to this New Age stuff was getting a bit heavy for him. Not the best cup of tea for a rational mind. But he refrained from making any comment and wondered where Lorne was heading.

"Think of how you and I ended up sitting here today," Lorne continued. "Was it really just a coincidence? Not in my opinion. Everything has meaning. I am in Lausanne for the first time in three months. You lose your sight. You make a random phone call. It ends up with me. I am available, I can come immediately. And in the space of just one hour, you have experienced being completely blind in full daylight while "seeing" a little of the non-obvious in the darkness. Don't you see the perfection in this? Isn't it possible to imagine that this was all guided?"

It was only then that Martin realized how much faith he had put into someone who was, after all, almost a complete stranger. Lorne's view of the world was bizarre. How could suffering be perfect?

Yet, in an unexplainable way, he felt there was some sense in what Lorne was saying. He wondered why he had not even tried phoning other people before Lorne arrived. Before he could think of any reason, a new thought struck him. It seemed a bit foolish, but there was no one else around to judge him anyway.

"If my body is the messenger …" Martin continued, saying his free-floating thoughts aloud, "then what is the unobvious … what is the real message?"

A faint shimmer.

Perhaps it was just Martin's imagination. He tried to concentrate harder. It was definitely a dark gritty image in shades of red. Would it stay with him? He relaxed his eyes for a moment. The grains were getting finer.

"Lorne! Wait …"

Suddenly, Martin found himself alert. Something was changing inside his head. An opening. A sensation like liquid flowing. It felt right. Was it his imagination?

Martin looked warily around.

He recognized the window-frames, the drawer in front of the bed and Lorne's silhouette sitting on the bed.

"My eyesight! I think it's coming back!"

Martin could see Lorne's shoulder-length hair, no longer in a ponytail like the last time he had seen him, but hanging straight down, almost touching his shoulders. His beige polo-neck jumper. A bright orange colour of something that could be the wristband of a watch.

It was for real.

Squinting, he looked round the bedroom again as if he were seeing things for the first time. Lorne asked him to imagine the healing process going on, the currents of energy travelling from an imaginary light-source inside his head.

"Try to take it on board," he said calmly. "Let your body do what it needs to do. Focus on your breath again."

Martin followed the particles of light travelling from his brain back towards the retina and felt how they gradually connected up with his nervous system. A heavy weight had been removed from his body, as though his fears and anxieties were being rinsed out.

Minute by minute, his sight was improving and Lorne phoned the hospital to inform Gabriella of the dramatic change in Martin's condition. Still shaken by what had happened, Martin wondered if it could be true. How could his blindness disappear so quickly and easily?

"You knew I would get my sight back, didn't you?"

"No. Honestly. But I am not surprised you did."

"But what happened? Was it because of the meditation or because of the blood-thinner that the doctor gave me? Was there a blood clot?"

Martin was getting tense again.

"Remember what we talked about. The visible and the invisible – the symptom and the underlying cause. Often we need to take the time to dig deeper if we want to find an explanation."

Martin thought for a little.

"I know what caused all this. The start-up. Just the thought of Attis makes me sick. That venture has been my curse. It's been one disaster after another."

Lorne looked out of the window, then at Martin.

"Everything in life is perfect. Even what we perceive as bad. I know it may sound strange to you right now, but this situation may end up being the best event that ever happened to you."

Martin sighed.

"You're losing me again, Lorne. Could we remain on ground level? Let me tell you one thing. All I have gone through, I don't want it *ever* to happen again."

"The situation with Attis contributed to triggering it all off. But was it really the main cause? If not, then whatever made you ill could come back in another form. Perhaps many years from now. Don't you want to find out about the origin of all this?"

"I don't know, Lorne. You're asking questions all the time."

"Isn't a good question better than a quick answer?"

Martin wished Lorne would use less cryptic language. He knew that something powerful had brought him to this critical point. What if Lorne was right and the situation with Attis was just the trigger?

"Perhaps you could start reflecting upon one important question: is there something I *don't* want to see?"

One of those damn questions again, like a pointed needle, stabbing right into his stomach. Martin wished Lorne would stop asking them. This one was irritating him a lot, but Martin couldn't say why.

"What is it that I don't want to see …?" He repeated while thinking. Right now he had absolutely no clue. He sensed that Lorne could not give him any further hints. But he had to find out, so as to prevent it coming back in some other nasty disguise.

Lorne stood up and got ready to leave.

"You should call Sarah," he said. "I spoke to her while you were sleeping. You're very lucky to have someone like her in your life. You two make a great couple."

Martin longed for Sarah more than ever. It had been an unbearable week without her. But he was worried he might hurt her again. And then it would definitely be over. He was not ready yet.

An important task remained. He had to go back and pick up where he had left off. The answer could be somewhere in the middle of it all, in the mess of Attis, like the needle in the haystack. There was just no way round it.

37

The Christmas decorations had been up for over a month now and roast-chestnut vendors were busy on the pedestrian street corners as people bustled around to find gifts for their loved ones.

Martin drove carefully through the sleet-covered streets of Lausanne. The pleasant atmosphere slowly drifted into his mind. After work, he would buy a present for Sarah.

He had spoken to her a couple of times on the phone. Long talks about the past and about their relationship. They had even laughed together. He had repeated the joke he always told people when they asked where he and Sarah had first met.

At the end of the world.

Puzzling, but true. That was where they had run into each other. Just outside Geneva, in the *Bout du Monde* forest. The forest at the end of the world.

He longed for Sarah to move back into the flat, but he was not ready yet. Perhaps in a couple of weeks, for Christmas. Maybe even later to make certain that he would not mess it all up again. Then he would be free to start anew.

When he thought about the situation in a level-headed way, things did look brighter all the same. His vision was back to its usual impeccable state and, just a week ago, he had managed to break free from the last chains of medication dependence. His good mood was not yet all that stable, however; it came and went like sunbeams from a sky full of fast-moving clouds. But he had also noticed that his feeling of happiness would linger on a little longer than before, even without the anti-anxiety pills.

In a few weeks' time, a new year would begin. Attis Therapeutics would no longer exist, putting an end to what seemed to be endless months of fundraising. He was so glad to be rid of that venture. A heavy burden was about to drop off his shoulders and he could begin the coming year with a clean sheet.

Martin reached the laboratories. As he parked the Clio, he thought of Lorne. A very strange person – but with interesting thoughts. The good resolutions he had made in front of Lorne were much easier to say than to keep. The nagging feeling of an unresolved issue had been hanging over him ever since.

Every day, Martin had expected some kind of sign that would show him the way forward in what he was supposed to do, but nothing came. Where would it come from? Would it just drop into his mind or on to his desk? Would he be able to recognize it when it eventually did come?

A grey Audi station wagon was parked on the other side of the street. It was Broccaz's car, with number plates from the Valais region. As discrete and efficient as the man himself.

This would be their last meeting and Martin was relieved not to have to deal with him any more. Broccaz had expressed no further interest in continuing the project. They had worked together for over a year now, but the fellow was still an enigma. What a strange, impenetrable personality. The old saying that 'nobody's perfect' was not true. Broccaz was the incarnation of flawlessness. Yet, at the same time, Martin sensed that it took powerful forces to hold it all together.

Well, he did not want to know about it anyway. It would soon all be history.

Tanya, Broccaz and Martin worked into the early afternoon on the papers. The planned shut-down of Attis was set for the last day of December; the patent rights for the drugs would revert to the university and probably become a basic research project again. In the future, perhaps someone with enough courage would attempt to raise money to restart a company. It was a pity that patients would not benefit until much later. Perhaps never. But Martin didn't care any more. Even about the money he had invested. It was just money after all.

A meagre thirty thousand would remain in the bank account after the last bills had been paid. Broccaz decided to make a gesture and suggested splitting the remaining money in three parts, although he had the contractual right to take it all.

Martin could still not believe it. In a little over a year, Broccaz had lost almost half a million Swiss francs but he did not appear to be the slightest bit annoyed. He had expected long debriefing sessions to find out what had gone wrong with the investors. Nothing like that at all. Perhaps the sum only meant a drop in a large ocean of money and activities.

While Broccaz was busy gathering up all his papers, Martin thought of what he had been through. He wanted to leave it all behind. Looking at Broccaz, he thought of the lab, the unexplained mycoplasma infection, the exploding ultracentrifuge, the vanishing investors.

At that same instant, Broccaz involuntarily caught Martin's glance, looked him in the eye for a moment, then turned his head away. One second off his guard, Broccaz had not stopped in time. An undefined sensation had shone through on a frequency invisible to the human eye, pure and undistorted.

Guilt?

Martin wanted to say something but, unable to find the words, he held back. Was Broccaz aware that he had involuntarily revealed something?

New kinds of questions started surfacing in Martin's mind. Could that far-fetched thought be true anyway? That this man had something to do with this failure?

He remembered the many times where his suspicions had run high; now he was no longer able to say whether they had been based on reality or a product of his growing paranoia.

Just because you're paranoid doesn't mean that they're not out to get you, Tom had once joked over a beer. Martin had laughed at the time, but right now, while he observed the inconspicuous, bespectacled man who was getting ready to say goodbye, he sensed that perhaps that saying did carry an element of truth.

As Martin shook Broccaz's hand, a question came into his mind. Why had he not thought of it earlier? The question was so perfectly simple, yet he had avoided asking it all the time.

Who are you, Mr Emile Broccaz?

Right now, he wanted nothing else from life than an answer to that question. Watching Broccaz leave, Martin tried desperately to think of what to do. This would be his last chance to find out more about this man. He could not ask him directly, but neither could he let him walk out the door, leaving the question unanswered. It was just not possible.

Martin stood up abruptly and picked up his coat. He vaguely heard Tanya talking from a distance, but did not listen to her. It was as if a new force had taken control of him. He hurried to the street door from where he could see Broccaz heading towards the Audi. As though in the simplistic plot of some dim-witted B-movie, he thought of tailing Broccaz's car. But follow him where? To his home? And then what?

He paused for a moment, realizing that he was about to embark on a very foolish undertaking. Everything told him that he was being completely ridiculous, but something stronger held him firmly to the idea. Where had all his reasonable behaviour during his tenure with Attis brought him? To the brink of catastrophe.

Why not find out where an impulse would take him?

38

The snow had stopped falling and the remaining sleet was almost gone from the roads. Fortunately, Broccaz was a prudent driver. The grey Audi headed towards the motorway and Martin decided to follow it from a safe distance, behind a couple of other cars. If he did lose sight of Broccaz, it would be easy to catch up with him again on the motorway.

He wondered where they were going and what would happen. Despite a natural inclination to dislike uncertainty, he now felt a surprising pleasure in not knowing what to expect. Earlier this week, he had read parts of a book that Sarah had once given him. After a few chapters, he had stumbled on an interesting formula: the happiness formula.

Happiness equals reality divided by expectations.

That might explain why, during the past year, he had felt less and less upbeat. Now that his expectations were close to zero, would the formula still hold?

The traffic on the wet motorway was quite light and Martin stayed behind a mini-bus to avoid being seen. They passed through several tunnels along the lake. He could see the rear lights of the Audi in front of the bus.

Did Broccaz have a house somewhere in the Valais? He certainly seemed to spend a lot of time out there. Perhaps he had a chalet for relaxing in during weekends. Martin had once tried to look him up in various directories, but the name 'Emile Broccaz' was not listed in any of them. Well, many people had secret addresses nowadays as a means of protection from other people. And Broccaz seemed particularly careful. He never wanted any documents sent to him and always came to the lab once or twice a week to pick them up.

After about an hour on the motorway, Broccaz turned off and started heading up the mountains on the left side of the valley. Martin knew the area slightly – it was about a half-hour drive from Sion where his parents lived.

The road had plenty of steep hairpin bends and he kept his distance. Halfway up, Broccaz turned off to the left and headed along a small forest road.

Martin slowed the car down on the main road and he heard several cars tooting behind him. He stopped and waved them by; he stayed there without moving for another few minutes before turning off. There were no other cars going on the tiny road Broccaz had taken, so he had to be very careful.

The gravel road with scattered patches of snow led through a forest of larch trees. Martin drove slowly to avoid the many deep holes in the road. Further ahead, the forest was thinner and the road became gradually more snow-covered. This was a place for a four-wheel drive, not a Clio. Martin decided to leave his car by the roadside, parked under two trees, and continued on foot. Wherever Broccaz was going could not possibly be much further. Did he really live in the middle of a forest? He did not seem to be that kind of person. Perhaps as a way of unwinding from his usual too-perfect demeanour?

He walked for another five minutes and noticed a sign written in red at the side of the forest road.

Propriété Privée.

That was it, Broccaz's residence. Did he live all by himself in there? Behind the gate, another gravel road seemed to disappear amongst the trees. That sign was not going to stop Martin. Now he wanted to find out. He walked past and climbed over the tall fence by the side with a thrilling sense of fearlessness.

Whoever you are Broccaz, I'll soon know. That'll be your Christmas present for me.

Martin could feel the melting snow starting to penetrate the leather soles of his shoes. He checked his watch. Close to four o'clock.

Suddenly, voices could be heard further ahead. He crouched down in complete silence. It sounded like a couple of men and one woman. What where they doing?

The whole situation felt awkward, but he decided anyway to move closer. Through the trees, he could see several houses built of wood. The main building looked like an old renovated farmhouse and behind it were several neat-looking chalets, all well-maintained. Outside the main entrance of the farmhouse, Martin observed three people in white coats smoking cigarettes. They finished off their cigarettes and went back in.

Martin took a deep breath. His curiosity was aroused. Were these people laboratory technicians or nurses? Impossible to say from this distance. It was probably some sort of clinic. He had to get closer. If this was not Broccaz's home, what was he doing in there? Was he being treated for some kind of disease?

Martin had to find out. But how? One possibility would be just to walk straight in, pretending innocently to be lost and ask plenty of naïve questions. Then, perhaps, he would get some answers. But trekking through a snow covered forest in loafers was not very credible. They would probably not tell him anything and then Broccaz would know. The chance would have been wasted.

It had to be done differently. With a chill of excitement running down his spine, he decided to move closer to the complex. He would be too visible if he approached the house through the front courtyard, so he decided to walk through the forest to see if there was a way in from behind.

Calls from crows in the woods were echoing back and forth as he moved slowly from tree to tree towards the rear of the farmhouse. From the edge of the forest, he could see that the farmhouse had a more recent extension towards the back, like some kind of garden conservatory; a man and a woman were sitting on a sofa, staring ahead as if they were watching a television programme. There was something unusual about them. They were both bald, with sunken eyes, and extremely thin. Their faces, with that gaunt prisoner-of-war look, seemed to be covered with yellow leather instead of skin.

He had obtained another answer. There was hardly any doubt about it. Broccaz was visiting a clinic with chemotherapy patients. But it was very odd that none of the oncologists he and Tanya had spoken to had ever mentioned this place. Did the authorities know there was a clinic right here? Perhaps just a small residence for patients recovering from chemotherapy? So why was there no sign on the road?

And why had Broccaz never told them about this place?

All of a sudden, the mobile phone in his pocket rang. He hastily managed to push the ignore button before it rang again and cursed himself for not putting it in silent mode earlier on. Luckily, he was still far away from the main entrance. He took a couple of pictures with the built-in camera before slipping the mobile phone back into his pocket. It vibrated, announcing another call, but he did not answer it.

What are you doing out here, Broccaz?

He heard the faint sound of a car engine, and men's voices again in the front courtyard. He walked back until he saw the silhouettes of Broccaz and another man. The two were carrying something that looked like a heavy container to the boot of an off-roader.

"Careful. Careful," he could hear Broccaz say.

Well, then, there was another answer. Broccaz had something to do with this clinic – and not as a patient. With his mobile phone, Martin took a short video of Broccaz and the other man, trying to zoom in as much as possible.

Suddenly it occurred to him that if someone from the clinic went back on the forest road, they would find his car. In no time at all, Broccaz would discover that he had been following him to this place. That thought was quite worrying. He had to get back to the Clio and leave.

Martin started running towards the gate, repeatedly slipping on the snow. For a moment, he thought he could hear footsteps behind him, and he ran faster. At the fence, he stopped and listened. There was no sound.

Relieved, he climbed over the gate and started sprinting down the forest road. As he reached the car, he turned round to listen again. The forest was very quiet and rather dark now. In five minutes, he would be back on the main road and that would be the end of today's excursion. What a weird trip it had been! Martin felt ill at ease thinking of it and was more than happy to return home.

He had seen a lot for one day. Some other time, he would come back without the car. Before that, a few friends he knew in the area could do a bit more investigating with the authorities.

I am going to find out who you are, Broccaz.

He took out his car keys and reached towards the door. Just as he got ready to sit down, a shadowy figure grabbed him hard from the side and pulled him out with tremendous force. Before Martin could turn round to see who it was, everything went black.

39

A few small containers with chemicals stood on the shelf above the bench in an almost empty laboratory. Apart from two refrigerators and the centrifuge, most of the instruments had been sold or given away. In just two weeks, a new start-up would take over Attis Therapeutics' facilities.

Tanya was alone in the lab. She glanced at the labels of the remaining chemicals while her thoughts kept turning back to the events in the lab office two hours earlier. She could still not understand what had happened during the session with Broccaz.

Towards the end of the meeting, Martin had appeared very different, completely beside himself, almost as if he were in some kind of a trance. That empty stare, so disturbingly full of an emotion she could still not define. Was it resentment? Hopelessness?

And the way Martin had left the office, in such a hurry, without even saying goodbye to her. Were they not supposed to debrief, to discuss what they had learned, like they did after every meeting? Had he behaved in this abrupt fashion because their dream, despite all the hard work and suffering, had just ended in huge disappointment?

She walked from the lab back to the office, wondering about the possible reasons and where Martin was right now. The legal documents they had signed were still on his desk. His shoulder bag still dangled from the back of the office chair. It all suggested his imminent return, except for one thing: the Clio was no longer in the parking space.

Things did not quite fit together – or did they?

Perhaps her emotions were carrying her away as well. The meeting had brought a little lump to her throat from time to time. Not only money and time had been invested in Attis – a lot of passion had been involved as well.

Relax, she thought. *Martin probably just wants to be alone for a little while. Let him digest things. Don't overreact.*

Later that afternoon, dispirited by the relentless silence of the office, Tanya resumed her search for explanations. She made several phone calls, but no one had heard from Martin. In the midst of another fruitless attempt to reach him on his mobile phone, a niggling voice inside her kept on saying that she had to take action. That Martin, in his still fragile state, had embarked upon a very thoughtless course of action with irreversible consequences.

Perhaps she was a little hysterical, but only finding him would calm her down. What could she do?

One after the other, she discarded the various options, irritated, blaming herself for not being able to fully tap into the usual swiftness of her mind.

Then the telephone rang next to her.

It was Sarah, returning her call.

After listening to Tanya's account of Martin's strange behaviour and sudden unexplained disappearance, Sarah knew that something was terribly wrong.

40

Martin woke up with his head throbbing and his throat excruciatingly dry. At first, he had no idea of where he was and what had happened. The back of his head hurt badly and he let out a little cry of pain as he touched it. Was this for real? Had somebody actually knocked him unconscious?

The pitch-blackness of the room brought back disturbing recollections of his terrifying loss of vision. He slowly pronounced a few cautious words, but they were thrown right back in his face, their edges sharp and unfriendly.

His fingers touched a cold, concrete floor.

What was this place? Who had brought him here?

With slow, awkward movements, he felt his way around the room. There was nothing else besides the mattress on the floor. The room was rather small and the door was bolted – a thick concrete door.

Martin felt nausea creeping up through his throat. The thought of being locked in was unbearable. He could not think freely, all his thoughts were trying to focus on a way to get out of this black cramped space.

Calm down. Calm down.

He had to control himself; otherwise, he would be overwhelmed by fear. He sat up against the wall and let his thoughts come rushing through. How had Lorne made him relax? Martin tried to recall the details. *Focus on your breathing.* He inhaled deeply and folded himself into an inner world of silence.

Everything is black, but you're still alive. Your body aches and your mind wants to panic but you know you can walk right through. The guide on the Kilimanjaro told you so on that last climb to the top. 'Pole-pole', slowly-slowly. You're breathing fine, slow regular breaths, not panting. The oxygen is there; breathe it in carefully. It's so steep right now that you want to give up, but instead you slow down. Focus on the length of your step. Make it short. You know you will get there. You always knew. Uhuru Peak. From there you can see everything. Even the sun shining like a bright flame in the darkness. From the highest point. Inside.

Suddenly the door was unbolted. A light was switched on in the room, but it was mostly useful for the person standing in the doorway. Martin squinted at the contours of the slightly-built man in front of him.

"Well, well. My dear Martin! I thought we were all set this morning. But it seems our paths continue to cross."

Broccaz's voice was surprisingly different, almost joyful.

"I don't understand," Martin said with bewilderment and felt the pain at the back of his head again.

"Why am I in here?"

Broccaz smiled.

"Would you agree with me that what you did was really *silly?*"

Broccaz made the word 'silly' sound like the most revolting word he had ever pronounced. He almost spat it out.

The whole scene seemed unreal to Martin. He was sitting on the floor like a schoolboy who had been trespassing through gardens in the neighbourhood, stealing apples, and now being punished to a degree that seemed completely disproportionate. What had he done?

"You see Martin, I don't like it when things get untidy."

"Untidy?"

Broccaz let out a long sigh.

"How on earth did you get this stupid idea of following me? I thought we finished everything that had to do with Attis Therapeutics? I even gave you some money back."

Martin did not know what to say. There was no rational explanation for what he had done. Nor for why he had been hit on the head. The whole situation was grotesque.

"Okay, since you're not much into talking today," Broccaz continued, "then I'll do it for you. I'm a great fan of privacy, you understand. That's why I live in Switzerland."

Broccaz was behaving strangely. His looks and gestures were communicating anger and yet, beneath it all, he seemed to be enjoying every single moment.

"Let me make an educated guess," he said. "You want to find out who's to blame for your recent miseries. Is that it? Well, you see, I'm afraid you have come to a dead end."

Broccaz produced a short burst of laughter that echoed all the way along the corridor.

"I'm not looking for scapegoats," Martin said. "Honestly. I imagine that I was just curious to find out who you are. My sincere excuses about following you, okay? But did you really have to knock me down for that? You could just have told me to leave."

Broccaz's suddenly looked very serious.

"Listen," Martin continued, "if my trespassing is such a big problem, then why don't you just call the police?"

He stood up from the mattress too suddenly. The next thing he noticed was a little dark handheld device that Broccaz pointed at his hip, followed by a powerful and painful shock and the surprising sensation of his leg muscles liquefying.

Seconds later, Martin was lying flat on his stomach on the mattress, held in a firm grip with both arms behind his back.

Unable to move, his nose deeply buried in the fabric and his arms starting to ache, he turned his head a little so he could speak.

"I ... Take it easy now! Why are you doing this to me? I wasn't threatening you in any way. What's wrong with you?"

Broccaz began tying Martin's hands together with adhesive tape. He did it thoroughly and without hurrying, as if he knew that Martin had given up any physical resistance. After finishing, he gave a final pull on the tape to test it.

"I know you inside-out, my nosy little friend. I know everything you have been doing, everyone you have talked to and every place you have gone to. And ..." Broccaz thought for a second, "it would not even be wrong to say that I control you."

Martin gasped for breath, wondering which parts of Broccaz's declarations were true and which were pure hallucinations. The fellow had the right to be angry, but the reaction seemed so absurdly exaggerated. Now he was even tied up! Talking over the situation like adults was probably not an option any longer. He had to get away from this man who was upset in a very unpredictable way.

"I know for instance that you have told no one about your trip here. That's good," Broccaz continued. "Very good indeed."

He let go of Martin's hands and stood up.

"Get up. We're going for a walk. You wanted some answers. Well, now it's time for you to get them."

41

Wailing sirens could be heard coming up the road. Moments later, an ambulance arrived in front of the emergency ward of the cantonal hospital of Lausanne. The driver and the emergency medical technician carried out a patient with an oxygen mask on a stretcher. They headed straight for the resuscitation area.

A young cleaner had phoned for the ambulance. She had finished her evening shift in the headquarters of an insurance company and was walking by a closed office, when she heard the sound of a man moaning faintly. On opening the door, she found him lying helplessly on the ground, shaking like a leaf and in a critical condition. He had seemed so thin and fragile that she wondered what kind of illness he was suffering from.

As one of the few still at work that evening, Menarti had been revising an urgent contract when a spear of pain had shot straight through his body; he collapsed immediately. Lying crumpled up in pain on the floor, he knew that something was terribly wrong. He had tried to shout for help but no words came out of his mouth. He had no breath left to carry them out. Just on the other side of his office door, the last people in the building were leaving as if nothing had happened. It was unbearable to know that life was going on without him just a few yards away when he did not have the strength to reach out for it – yet, just a little while ago, he was part of it all. For half an hour, he lay on the floor, not far from them, fighting a lonely battle for his life. Yet none of them heard him.

Lying on the stretcher in the emergency ward of the hospital with scores of doctors and nurses rushing about, Menarti desperately tried to fight against the heaviness invading his thorax and the terrifying fear that gnawed at him. He had been here before, twice this year, in that universe of great pain. Why was his heart giving up now? Why would God save him twice just to let him die anyway? That was absurd.

His mind was still working with surprising clarity. Had he gone back to work too soon? Should he have listened more to Broccaz, to his own wife and family who had told him to take a long rest? But not working at all would have been fatal for him as well.

It felt as though his chest was welded together into one solid mass, and every tiny movement he made hurt him terribly. He fought against losing consciousness, because he knew that if the blackness won, it would all be over.

Menarti could still sense that the doctors, now very far away, were doing all they could to revive him. Drugs were injected into his arm and he was rushed to an operating theatre where he could vaguely sense the electric current passing through his chest. But he was leaving it all, slowly sinking into the darkness that seemed to evolve into a big deep lake. This time, he knew he was not coming back. There was no more oxygen. And then the pain went away too.

42

Broccaz got Martin to his feet on the floor of the little room and pushed him out into the dimly lit underground corridors.

With his arms tied behind his back and his legs still wobbly from the electric shock, Martin began to sway; he was just about to stumble when Broccaz grabbed hold of his arms.

"It's funny, you know. When you stagger like that … it reminds me of a marionette."

Martin was too unsettled to reply, wondering what kind of layout was awaiting him. "Listen …" he said nervously. "Please. Just tell me what you want from me."

"What I want from *you*?" Broccaz stopped. "My dear Mr Rieder. I think you're getting it all wrong now. You're reversing the roles. Remember, you wanted something from me. Rest assured, you *will* get it."

Martin cursed the flash of curiosity he had had that afternoon in the office. It had been hasty and so damn foolish, but now he knew it was too late to turn away from whatever it was that Broccaz had in mind for him.

"Walk with me," Broccaz whispered full of enthusiasm.

Martin's legs would not obey. After a few clumsy steps, he fell. Broccaz caught him by the arms and jerked them upwards. An excruciating pain shot up through his shoulders and he groaned in agony while still on his knees.

"I'm afraid you'll have to get used to walking in this unbecoming way. It's best for you to be tied up, you see. Then I don't have to use this device on you again."

Broccaz looked at his watch. He grabbed hold of a backpack on the floor and flung it around one shoulder.

"Now get up. It's time for the exciting part. We could call it the *happy hour* if you like."

Advancing through the maze of corridors, they passed a number of light panels and a hall with a staircase leading upstairs. Martin tried to make a mental note of it all, but Broccaz walked briskly and made so many left and right turns that Martin quickly lost his sense of direction.

They reached a door with a face recognition system and Broccaz stopped in front of it.

"You've been a good contributor to my project so I think you deserve to see this technological wonder. In fact, you're among the very few people who will ever see *all* of it."

He bent forward, pushed a button and the red stroboscope beam scanned his face. For a few seconds, the whole corridor was filled with a flickering red light; then a voice confirmed his right to access, giving the place a chilly atmosphere.

"Ready, my young friend?"

The concrete door slid to one side.

Martin had never seen such an expression on Broccaz's face. His small eyes were sparkling like dark-grey diamonds in the sparse light.

"May I introduce you to the creation of my life?" Broccaz gestured and switched on the neon light.

The sight was astounding.

Eight black man-height monolith-shaped computers with ribbed surfaces stood on the floor of the large concrete room. They were arranged in an odd asymmetrical pattern, like items of modern art in a gallery.

"They are marvellous, aren't they? You like the way I have set them up? I never leave anything to chance. Like the chalets upstairs, they're organized so that they resemble a flying swan when you see them from above. A beautiful black swan. Heavenly aren't they? Here, look. Try to look at them from over there."

With a swift movement, Broccaz pushed Martin towards the corner of the room.

"Like it?"

Martin nodded in silence. He would have to be ready for the right opportunity to escape. That was his only chance. A moment of inattention on Broccaz's part and he would go for it. He would run back to find the staircase leading up to the ground floor. He wondered if such a moment would come and whether his legs would do their duty. They felt better, but it was hard to say in what sort of shape the lean man was. If Broccaz was the one who had pulled him out of the car with such amazing force, then Martin had a lot to be worried about.

"It's not only art, you see," Broccaz said, "I suppose you know what a computing power of eight Teraflops means?"

Martin hardly listened while he thought of possible escape plans.

"Eight trillion calculations per second! Can you imagine the kind of computing power that represents? I can expand it in the future with more processors, but I don't think it will be necessary – even with new Windows releases."

Broccaz forced a short laugh at his own joke, probably also rehearsed to perfection.

"It would easily make it to the top 500 supercomputer list in the world. But no one, apart from you and me and a few experts, know about its existence. Don't you find that … thrilling?"

"What's it for?" Martin asked, to keep Broccaz talking. He looked carefully for anything that would facilitate an escape attempt. With his hands taped behind his back, the only possibility would seem to be a well-aimed kick at Broccaz. He had to play for time and hope for a moment of inattention.

"Why all this computing power?"

Broccaz proudly explained the Carnivore project.

"The world has so much biological information to offer, but you know what?" he said with excitement. "No one makes universal sense of it. Except God".

He thought for a brief moment and continued light-heartedly: "But now even God's got some serious competition. You know, Carnivore is really about finding new ways to cure cancers that those hopeless – those imbecile – doctors have given up on. I have cured many patients that were abandoned by them – and abandoned by God as well for that sake. I am reversing the course of events. I am winning the fight against death."

Martin did not like his choice of words. The controlled façade was gone and instead of the courteous banker, he caught a glimpse of a man possessed. Broccaz was now openly sharing the secret of his life's work with a prying sightseer who had come off the beaten track. That did not augur well for things to come. He had to keep his fear under control.

Focus on now.

"What do you think of that, Martin? Isn't that a bit different from Attis Therapeutics? A different playing field, eh? Well, in all honesty, you should know that Attis was very useful to me."

He put on a smile that did not fit at all.

"Actually, you were a pretty good guinea pig for Carnivore."

Broccaz began to explain, but Martin could not listen. It was too painful to realize that for the whole of the last year, many of the things he had to endure were just part of a carefully planned set-up. That he had been misled, pushed and hijacked away from his dream.

"The mycoplasma infection and the centrifuge explosion. You did that?!" The rage boiling up inside Martin overcame his stifling fear. Why had he not trusted, or at least investigated, his own first intuitions?

Broccaz smiled. "The investors were surprisingly easy to scare away, you know. Much easier than Professor Larousse."

Martin was fuming with anger, mostly against himself. He clenched his teeth and sensed the tape tied round his hands behind his back.

"To hell with you!" he shouted. "Whatever supernatural being you believe you are! You're just ... bloody mad."

"I shall take that as a compliment," Broccaz said with contentment. "Madness and genius. They're really two sides of the same coin."

He walked over and put an arm around one of the monolith computers.

"Look at these! Then look at yourself. By any kind of objective measure, you have achieved absolutely nothing. You see, when you want to be successful, the name of the game is control. That's where you went wrong, Martin. Even if I had not intervened, sooner or later, you would have run into disaster anyway. Not because you're weak, not because you're unintelligent, but because you let everyone do their own thing."

Broccaz pushed him into an adjoining room full of computer screens.

"This is my place for doing just that. My control room. And believe me, I control absolutely everything from here."

Martin saw his mobile phone lying on the table. Going directly over to one of the screens, Broccaz seemed to ignore it at first. He scrolled the computer mouse, clicked an icon and a map appeared with a little blinking triangle.

"See that little symbol? That's your mobile phone tracer. It didn't take me long to find out you were here."

Broccaz typed in a number on the keyboard, picked up the mobile phone and spoke into it. His voice came out clearly on a pair of speakers on the desk.

"Long-range listening device as well. Amazingly simple to set up. But now it's no longer necessary."

He looked at the mobile phone for a short moment, turned away from the table and with a swift movement threw the phone against the concrete wall. An amplified crash came from the speakers and echoed down the corridors.

"We're getting towards the end of the sightseeing tour. You'll like this last room."

Another face recognition system barred the entry to a large hall, which was full of activity. As they entered, Martin recognized the massive pipetting robots that he had only seen once before, on a visit to a big pharmaceutical company laboratory.

"So, what do you think? Is this madness too?" Broccaz said. "Brute force, working twenty-four hours a day at incredible speed. No mycoplasma infections in here – ever!" he said with a twinkle in his eye.

Martin had to keep it all in, even though he badly wanted to hit this perverted man.

"You … pathetic bastard!" he shouted. "I bet that, in her grave, your mother is regretting that she ever brought a sick thing like you into the world!" Martin went on. "You think you can control everything. Well, for one thing, you don't control me."

Broccaz coughed slightly to clear his throat before Martin ended his sentence. It was as if he pretended not to hear the first part of what had just been said. The jaw muscles just below his ear twitched. But then he smiled and regained his composure. Martin had given him the appropriate cue for what would happen next.

"You really believe that? I don't control you, eh? Let me make a suggestion then: how about we put that little theory to the test?"

It was all very unfortunate that Martin had come here, but even with this unexpected visit, Broccaz had everything planned within a few hours. He knew of only one solution to this irrevocable situation. A life had to be taken. Not an easy task, but there was no other way. Still, the plan had one glitch that annoyed him. He had searched everywhere for possible solutions and eventually he found one. In a book on human psychology.

43

Broccaz led his prisoner back through the tunnels towards the staircase they had passed. Before going up the steps, he cut off a fresh strip of adhesive tape and stuck it over Martin's mouth.

"Just a precaution. It wouldn't be a good thing for my patients to hear any screaming around here. They come from all over the world, you know. I don't want anyone to lose faith in my clinic."

Broccaz stopped at the bottom of the staircase.

"Almost every month, I cure a terminal cancer patient. Over time, that makes a lot of lives," he said dreamingly. "All those clueless oncologists would envy me if they knew. Wouldn't it be fair to say that the universe owes me a little favour? Wouldn't you say so, Martin?"

He fell silent and studied the expressions that passed over Martin's face.

"You give many and you take one," Broccaz said slowly.

Martin's blood turned cold.

He could not believe what he had just heard.

Take one?

Perhaps he had not heard right. Or perhaps Broccaz was just saying it to scare him. That fellow was capable of anything. Martin was looking at a big dark wall, too smooth to climb over, with no door to let him through. There was no way out. He felt as though he were suffocating and wanted to scream but the tape over his mouth only let through an insignificant little mumble.

Broccaz reached for the backpack, opened it and took out a handgun.

"Now. We need to get going."

He pushed Martin up the staircase. Demoralized, but with his body on red alert, Martin felt his legs moving forward mechanically. If he tried to run away, Broccaz might pull the trigger. Upsetting a few patients, woken up in their expensive beds, was a price that Broccaz was probably ready to pay. Martin had no fight left in him any more. He was so small. So insignificant.

They reached the hall of the main building. It was dark and quiet outside and the reception area seemed empty. Broccaz went behind the desk and took out a pair of gloves and a rope. Then he grabbed Martin's arms, still taped behind his back, and pushed him through the courtyard towards the parking lot. It was only when they were right in front of it that Martin realized that his Clio was among the cars. Broccaz opened the door, pushed him into the passenger seat, and tied him firmly to it with the rope.

"We're going for a little drive. You see, sooner or later, we all have to sacrifice ourselves for a higher cause."

A profound sense of fear was beginning to seep into Martin's brain.

Could this really be true? Were there no avenues open to him now? Was this the end?

The full moon was barely visible behind a thin veil of clouds that covered most of the sky as they left the parking lot. The car headlamps lit up the bumpy dirt road; Broccaz drove very fast. The engine revved loudly.

"You're wondering where we're going?" Broccaz asked as he shifted the gears up and down in the bends. "Not far now. Here, let me take that thing off."

With a quick pull, he removed the tape from Martin's mouth.

Sitting in his own car had eased away a little of Martin's panic. The familiar surroundings and the fact that he could breathe more freely gave him some slight relief. Like a tiny oasis in the vast desert of dread.

He tried to push forward, but the rope kept him tied tightly to the seat. Broccaz had left nothing to chance. Was this really his mission in life? To be sacrificed by a madman? Time was running out. Could he talk some sanity into him?

"Listen. If I die, the police will investigate and your name will come up. You'll be on the list of suspects. That could become dangerous for your outfit up here. Do you really want to risk that?"

Broccaz did not reply, nor did he look at Martin.

The road became narrower and branches were rubbing against the car on both sides. He was still driving fast, but had the car under control. The headlamps jumped up and down.

"You know Farinet?" Broccaz asked.

Martin's taped arms, trapped between his back and the seat, were beginning to hurt.

"I imagine you do. Everybody in this part of Switzerland knows him. Farinet. The Robin Hood of the Alps. What a fellow!" he said and laughed.

"A saint and a scoundrel. Such a pity he died a hundred years ago. If he were still alive today, I could have run into him up here. We would have been brothers-in-arms. Such an interesting man, you know. Farinet refused to play the fake game of society. He scorned all its rules and used every means to reach his goal. Manipulated people. Made his own counterfeit money and gave it to the poor."

The car hit a hole in the road and the suspension did little to cushion the impact. Their heads almost hit the roof of the car. Broccaz slowed down a little.

"Did you know that the police caught him several times but that he always managed to escape from prison? They couldn't keep him locked up. He managed to live his entire life above the law. He was free."

Broccaz nodded slowly as he looked out of the window.

"That's how I see myself. Living above the law, and at the same time doing good. Farinet helped desperately poor people by giving them money. I help desperate people too. I give them life."

They reached a fork in the road; instead of going back towards the main road, Broccaz turned right along another gravel road. The car skidded as it went round the bend, but he counter-steered, then accelerated as if he were about to kill them both.

With adrenaline coursing through his veins, Martin tried to keep a cool head in the hope of finding a way out of this nightmare.

"I'm taking you to a very special place. It's so beautiful there. You'll see. It all fits so very perfectly together."

They drove for another few endless minutes and arrived at a clearing near the edge of the forest. Martin could just make out the vineyards below. They were close to the mountainside and a faint shimmer of light came from the villages down in the valley. Broccaz stopped the car and turned off the headlamps. He untied Martin and waved him out with the gun in his hand.

The moon peeked through the cloud cover; there was no wind to move the bare branches. The only sound that could be heard came from a stream further down. Broccaz went round to the back of the car and took the backpack out of the boot.

Now Martin realized where they were. All his panic came flooding back. The narrow wooden beams, the steel wires, the large white dove sculptured on the mountain wall, the strange feeling of being drawn to the depths below.

The Passerelle de Farinet. Farinet's footbridge. Swaying gently, high above the gorge.

Broccaz took the knife out of the backpack and pushed Martin towards the bridge, which was partly lit up by the moon. With a few quick cuts, he removed the tape that bound Martin's hands.

"They say that Farinet was a handsome young man. About your age when he died."

He pushed Martin onto the bridge and pointed with the gun into the gorge. "They found him dead right down there. Even today no one knows whether he was killed by the police or if he committed suicide."

Martin stopped.

The final part of Broccaz's devilish plan was beginning to dawn on him. He tried to speak but the words stuck in his throat. Oh please, help. Someone.

"Broccaz. You don't want to do this. Please. I'll keep the secret, I promise." Martin's voice was trembling. "You know … for me to commit suicide right now, that wouldn't make sense. People know that I'm feeling better. I stopped taking medication. I want to live. My friends know that and they'll say so to the police. People will never believe that I killed myself."

Broccaz's voice changed. It had the unflinching tone of an experienced lecturer standing in front of a full auditorium.

People suffering from severe anxiety and depression frequently have suicidal thoughts and they may even attempt suicide. But they are mostly too weak to act. The critical period is when they feel their spirits and energy rising. When they tell everyone that they will be fine and they seem well on the way to recovery. At that very moment, according to the statistics, the ability and willingness are at their highest level. To carry out the act.

44

It was shortly after midnight when Sarah anxiously unlocked the door to the flat from which she so hastily had moved out three weeks ago. Minutes earlier, she had rung the doorbell with such intensity that a neighbour had come up the stairs to see what was happening. But the person she so badly longed for had not appeared after several rounds of ringing. Instinctively Sarah knew that something was wrong and she could tell that Tanya, who was standing beside her, was thinking exactly the same.

Inside the flat, they were met by the mess and odours of a busy man who had only recently begun to learn the art of living alone. Dirty clothes, unwashed dishes, bottles with leftovers of different substances, the stuffy smell of old coffee and sweat clinging to the rooms that begged for a window to be opened. Everything smelled of stress and withdrawal. They ran through all the rooms, but Martin was nowhere to be found.

Where have you gone, sweetheart? Sarah thought with concern. *Please tell me.*

Was there anything unusual in here, anything that could point to where he was? Sarah glanced at the painting of the old lighthouse on the wall above the sofa. It brought back the last awful moments of their argument and break-up. She felt sorry for Martin and badly regretted leaving him, but right now her priorities were different. Nothing else mattered more than seeing him, even just hearing his voice saying that he was doing fine.

Tanya had noticed that the diary Martin had left behind in the lab office was blank for the afternoon and the following days. Whatever he was up to now had not been planned in advance. *Or had it?*

Where could he have gone? Why hadn't he said anything? And, more worryingly, why was the mobile phone he always took with him now suddenly switched off?

It all seemed so unlike him.

They began a meticulous search for clues throughout the flat. A note, an unusual item, a missing bag. Anything would do. Anything that could give them the tiniest hint of where he might be.

While Tanya pushed the replay-button on the answering machine, she told Sarah about Martin's strange behaviour in the office at the end of the meeting with Broccaz. It only added to Sarah's worries and she ran to the bathroom and searched the cabinet where she knew Martin kept his medication. Feverishly, she grabbed hold of bottles and blister packs and scattered them across the bathroom table. She found the sleep medication, but where were the anti-anxiety pills? The dreadful thought, however distant, of Martin committing suicide was slowing creeping in on her without her being able to fully accept it.

Then she saw something that made her blood go cold. On top of a full waste-paper basket on the floor was an empty anti-anxiety pill blister pack.

Oh, Martin, where are you? Please don't do anything desperate.

Feeling helpless, Tanya and Sarah sat down on the sofa. They had no idea where he had gone, but they looked at each other, knowing full well that something had gone terribly wrong. After another rundown of the few remaining options, it was clear that they had no other choice but to call the police.

But how would a police officer react to a search request for an adult person who had gone missing for just half a day? And what tangible proof did they have that something had happened to him?

They knew the answer in advance.

Ahead of them lay a long, gruelling night of waiting.

45

With each step they took towards the middle of the footbridge, the wooden beams swayed a little and Martin came closer to fainting from fear. The moon shimmered between the clouds, bathing the long, narrow bridge in a fine, almost secretive yellow light while the stream trickled on its course through the gorge far down below.

"You know, Martin. I do care a lot about you." Broccaz stared down the gorge for a moment as if in a trance. He turned round to face him.

"Much more than you could possibly understand."

Despite Broccaz's efforts to appear calm and composed, Martin could see that something else besides madness was at work inside him.

"People can be scary. That's why I used to keep away from them. I still do most of the time, but now I'm afraid of nobody. People know instinctively that I'm in control. They eat out of my hand. Like puppets. So powerless and miserable. Writhing so much that it's almost funny."

Broccaz coughed from time to time, but his voice remained calm. The gun was still nestling in his left hand.

"You know what life is about? It's about rising above ordinary people. You see, ordinary people, they all feel limited in their life. They complain, but they do nothing about it. Numbed by it all, they walk unconsciously towards what they fear most. They stroll straight into death."

His eyes widened. "I'm just the opposite, you see. I am free. I do whatever I want. I prolong life like no other human being. And I no longer fear death."

Martin could not find anything to say. Was this his body's way of preparing for the end? The chicken heading for the slaughterhouse? In a few minutes, he would be dead. And he was just going to wait for it to happen? There had to be something worth living for.

"Why do you have to kill *me*?"

Martin could hardly recognize his own words that came out as a bleak shriek.

Broccaz looked at his gun in a brief moment of thoughtful silence.

"Your life has crossed mine in a very unfortunate and irrevocable way. We can't turn the clock back. The world is still not ready to understand my work. That I *have* to break the law to save dying people. And now, well … it's all too late."

Martin was starting to panic, adrenaline flowing stronger. There was so little time left. He had to do something. A last negotiation for his life.

But nothing came into his mind, except rage.

"You're crazy!" he shouted, much louder than before. "You're living in your own mad dream-world!"

Broccaz took off his backpack and put it on the ground.

"Enough! Discussion over," he said with determination and took a step forward. "We need to get on with the last part, Martin."

Broccaz pointed the gun straight at Martin's face.

"So, here's what you'll do. Climb up on to that handrail and jump. It is much easier than you think. Especially if you do it swiftly, without any hesitation. Look, there, just between those two wires. Trust me. I want to do what ultimately is best for you. It'll relieve you from all your problems. So that you can be free."

Martin was rooted to the spot. That strange, yet familiar, sensation of being drawn towards the depths. It would be terribly easy.

"Why do you want to go on suffering?" Broccaz continued. "You've lost everything that matters to you, haven't you? Your girlfriend, your business partner, your company, your job, your hopes … Isn't that a sign that things should be coming to an end? What holds you back from taking the final step? Your lack of courage?"

Martin could not think clearly any longer. Everything was muddled together. Perhaps Broccaz was right anyway. Perhaps it was all supposed to end like this. He was too tired to fight. *Not heart disease, not cancer, oh no. Life! That damned life is the biggest killer of them all.*

"Go on. Get it over with, Martin."

Broccaz put his finger on the trigger.

For a brief moment, Martin felt as if the footbridge was swaying a little more forcefully above the ravine, despite the strong wires that stabilized it. A coarse, slow tremor pulled him out of his daze. Was there someone else here? He glanced in both directions, but the path was completely empty.

"Come on. Now!" Broccaz said, firmly.

What would be worse? To be killed by a bullet or a hundred-metre free fall? Why was Martin thinking of that right now when he couldn't care less? Tomorrow it would not matter anyway. Not to him. But Broccaz had still not pulled the trigger. Would he really be prepared to do it?

"You … you," Martin stuttered. "You've got it all wrong … you can't save lives and kill people. It doesn't make sense."

Barely visible in the moonshine, a slight frown appeared on Broccaz's face.

"I can do whatever I want," he hissed. "Now, go on, jump!"

Broccaz still looked composed, but the tone of his voice had changed in a subtle way.

Things are often different from what they appear to be, Lorne had said back in the flat when Martin had called him in despair. He had to fish for another explanation. A different angle. Like a scientist. *Search for it. The needle in the haystack.*

"That Carnivore project. You sacrificed your life and money. Not to help people. You did it out of guilt, didn't you?" His breath coming quickly, Martin spoke in one final attempt to hold Broccaz back. "To make yourself feel all-powerful."

Broccaz stopped, his head tilted sideways, warningly.

Had Martin touched a raw nerve? He had to find the link. To continue.

"It must have been unbearable," he said, fumbling his way through an unknown territory, "with your mother dying and you being unable to help her. Carnivore prevents you from feeling helpless, doesn't it? You think you're God, but its only to hide your fear of losing control."

Broccaz shook his head with a broad smile, regaining his equanimity.

"First year psychology theories … Nice try, Martin! Doesn't work on me. Now, stop trying to buy more time … be a man and get it over with."

Another dead-end. There had to be a solution. Where was that other part of the iceberg? What if Broccaz had built his life around another pattern?

Everything began to tremble. A slideshow with each frame appearing after the other, flickering from side to side. So unbearably fast. Broccaz. The footbridge. The illuminated darkness. The edge of the unknown.

What was happening? Was he going mad as well?

He had to keep on talking.

"What would your beloved mother think of you right now? You trying to keep control by killing me!"

"Beloved." Broccaz repeated with a sudden flat-eyed stare.

The word came like a slap in Martin's face. He felt light-headed. Like in those first few moments when a scientist discovers something new. Living on the edge of what you don't know, working with methods that are no longer good enough and then, all of a sudden, to be the first to discover the internal workings of an organism that everyone else keeps watching from the outside.

Suddenly he knew.

"You hated her! You hated your mother!"

"Rubbish ..." Broccaz mumbled.

In that very moment Martin knew he was onto the truth. It was the only thing he remained certain of. The harsh, dreadful truth.

"You wanted to hurt her all your life, didn't you?" Martin shouted with eagerness. Words just kept on streaming out of his mouth.

"Even to kill her. But you just couldn't do it, right Emile? No guts to kill her. But then, luckily, she got cancer and you saw your chance. You didn't want her to get early treatment that could have saved her! How did you make her wait? By preventing her from seeing those imbecile oncologists, huh?"

Broccaz's expression gave a fuller answer than words could ever provide.

"And ever since, you made yourself believe a different story. That the doctors killed her. But deep inside, you always knew the truth. And now you have to save patients' lives to make up for killing her. You don't want blood on your hands, right? Sickness killed your mother and suicide is to be my fate, eh? Always twisting the truth to suit your reality. You're totally insane!"

A brief fit of shivers ran through Broccaz's body.

That was the moment Martin needed. It had come. The door in the wall of death. Time – a few fractions of a second – interrupting the nightmare he had succumbed to.

Instinctively he bent down and reached for Broccaz's feet, expecting to hear and feel the life-ending bullet shooting out of the gun barrel. But surprisingly it did not come, no numbing pain hit him either. The stream continued its distant slow-motion flow as both his hands grabbed the brown corduroy trousers, sensing the thin, wiry ankles underneath, pulling them upwards.

Instead of a heavy weight, he found a different kind of quality, something much lighter than he had expected. He yelled louder than he had ever done before as Broccaz's feet left the wooden beams of the footbridge and came up into the air with such little resistance, so unexpectedly high up, as if gravity had ceased to exist. There was a faint sound of a bang somewhere, echoing through the gorge, but it was already far away. Martin did not know if it was the gun or whether he had been hit by a bullet. He continued his relentless upward movement, driven by something he was no longer in command of.

Broccaz's face appeared on the other side of the handrail, eyes wide open, before he rolled over and down into the depths. His body disappeared silently into the gorge; he did not utter a single scream all the way down. The impact as he hit the ground far below sounded almost soft and was quickly swallowed up by the noise of the river.

46

Shivering in the cold, his ears still ringing from the blast of the gun, Martin clutched the handrail of the footbridge and stared down into the darkness of the gorge as if he were expecting Broccaz to re-emerge.

Was Broccaz dead?

No one could survive a fall of over a hundred metres down into a ravine full of rocks. Yet, it still appeared so unreal. The sequence of events had happened with incomprehensible speed.

Had he really taken the life of a human being?

All Martin could think of was that he had somehow acted in self-defence.

What was that last look he saw in Broccaz's eyes?

Relief?

He sat down on the beams of the footbridge, breathing quickly, trying to gather his thoughts.

The details of the plan for his so-called suicide began slowly to emerge. It was a very clever plan indeed. Now he understood why they had come here in the Clio. The police would find it next to the bridge and assume that he had driven it up from Lausanne during the last desperate moments of his life. The keys were probably still in the car.

Martin tried to recall the moment when he had managed to gather all his inner strength together and make a grab for Broccaz's legs.

Why had he fallen without offering any resistance at all? Why would a man who had so maliciously built up his clandestine experimental research facility and planned everything down to the tiniest detail let go of it all just like that?

To Martin, it just did not make sense.

There was another, even more mysterious possibility.

Could it be that Broccaz had let himself being pushed off the bridge of his own free will? That the suicide he had so meticulously planned was in fact quite simply ... his own? That he needed Martin's help with the final part of the plan because he did not have enough courage to go all the way?

No one would ever know. Broccaz had taken the secret away with him down into the depths of the gorge.

A profound sense of melancholy and emptiness crept over Martin, almost as if a part of him had fallen over the railing with Broccaz.

He wanted to get away from the place.

It was probably better to go straight to the police, but he was in too confused a state to stand up to an interrogation. There was a risk that he'd say things he'd regret later.

In the moonlight, he walked across the bridge away from his car, towards the forest. He followed a small path without really knowing where he was heading. It was rather dim, but his eyes adapted and he could see a little in the faint light; he could make out a narrow trail leading downwards. It was strange to be walking through the forest in the middle of the night, yet he felt somehow connected to the comforting silence that surrounded the trees.

As he came out of the woods, he could see below him the lights of the villages down in the valley. The first had to be Saillon. He started to run down the path between the sloping vineyards as fast as his legs could carry him.

Just before the village, a sign caught his attention. He stopped to read it. It said *Sentier de Farinet*, Farinet's path. He knew the place it was leading to – a very special vineyard. Many times in the past he had thought of coming here, but for some reason, he had never done so, in spite of the fact that he had grown up nearby. Perhaps it was because, at that time, vines were just vines to him. There were more than enough of them at his parents' estate.

Now he wanted to explore this very particular spot. He began walking up towards *la Colline Ardente*, the glowing hill, as it had been named in honour of Farinet.

The hill was quite unremarkable, just a few trees on top and vines growing on the slopes on each side. The remaining leaves had fallen off the plants during the recent snowfall, so that the fields were covered in long rows of dark, naked stalks.

Martin could just make out the contours of Saillon with its many roofs all huddled together. In the houses, adults and children were sleeping quietly in their beds, ignorant of the human drama that had just taken place in the mountains above them.

He did not particularly want to see anybody. He preferred to stay up in this little hideout for a while, sheltered from the outside world.

A narrow path, *l'Allée de l'Immortalité,* which had a roof of vines growing on metal bars that curved to form an arch, led the way up to the plateau of the hill. Martin stood at the entrance and looked up the path. The low stone walls on either side of the alley were covered in many-coloured plaques carrying ex-voto messages that visitors had hung up over the years – about freedom, about Farinet, about hope, about many other things in life. There was enough light, but Martin did not feel like reading them. Suddenly, a little white plaque with a few lines etched on it caught his eye and held his attention.

With perceptions so deeply twisted by reality
We sometimes need to lose ourselves
In order to find the way

Slowly he began to walk up the alley.

An unlimited space was beginning to unfold inside his body, allowing his thoughts to circulate freely. Each step he took up the alley gave him the impression that the entire place was vibrating with a special kind of force. Never before had he felt such intensity in the Valais – or anywhere else, for that matter.

What was it in this place that was having such an effect on him? Making him forget the world around him and the last frightening hours he had spent with Broccaz?

Tears began streaming down his face. He just could not hold them back. He sensed a new certainty, not the knowing kind, but the type of certainty that arises when powerful bonds are built up. He sat down on a stone for a while, wiping his face with his sleeve. Things would be all right. He had no idea why, he just knew. Something, whatever it was, had given way, irrevocably.

After a few minutes, Martin stood up and took a deep breath. It was time to walk the last part of the way to the top. To mark the end of the anguish he had gone through. Only then could he come back to face the world – but with a renewed appetite. And, more than anything else right now, he wanted to be with his family.

On the plateau, he reached a very unusual vineyard. Each stem carried a different name-tag, that of its owner. Martin climbed on to the wall to have a closer look. Hundreds, perhaps even thousands of name-tags. Famous people had come to visit this hiding place and bless its vines: Mother Teresa, Roger Moore, Michael Schumacher. He walked round them, from one stem to another, slowly reading every name.

These vines seemed to carry something other than mere grapes. They had another quality, the ability to provide a refuge for anybody seeking a little freedom from life. Because that was what life was all about, wasn't it? Finding that tiny hidden retreat to renew yourself when you could no longer unearth one inside.

Further on, Martin crouched down in front of a separate little vineyard, nestling humbly on one square metre of land. A little sign said that it was the smallest registered vineyard in the world, with only three stems altogether. And that it belonged to the Dalai Lama.

Epilogue

Four months had passed and a crisp spring sun was setting over the garden of the Falcroft estate. Sarah's hard-working landscaping team had transformed it into a park of extraordinary beauty. Plants and shrubs were organized into enclaves of biotopes and paths, each holding its own little secret. The first flowers had ventured out in their beds. Fluorescent blue grape hyacinths, yellow forsythias, velvet-red primroses.

Lorne sat with Martin on a quiet bench in front of a Japanese-styled pond with small islands made of stones. Neither of them spoke as they watched the white and red Koi-fish winding their bodies through the water.

They had met on several occasions, mostly without other people around. Martin always felt he entered a different world when he was with Lorne, a world he did not want to share with anyone else. It was not an escape, rather a detachment from the dramatic events that still seemed as though they had occurred only days ago.

Many things had happened after the scary night on the footbridge.

The police had recovered Broccaz's body shortly after Martin had notified them at dawn on that frosty December morning. Soon after, the Swan clinic was seized and ever since, the local authorities had been busy figuring out what to do with all its valuable assets.

The interrogation of Martin had been tough, but in his mind, while answering the many questions, he was still somewhere on top of that hill with all the name-tagged wine-stems, bathed in its remarkable glow. During some very difficult moments at the beginning of the year, when Martin had suffered from renewed bouts of guilt, he had gone up to visit the hill, looking for the plaque he had read on that occasion. There were so many of them, but, strangely enough, none carried the message he had seen.

Martin sighed and looked ahead into the dark water of the pond.

"What a bloody awful year. I just want to forget all about it. I hope that I'll never experience anything like it again. Ever!"

"It's all about interpretation, isn't it?"

"What is?"

"Life."

Martin picked up a little stone and threw it into the water. Several fish came rushing towards the place where it had landed.

"Martin, you're certainly free to see yourself as a victim during the events you went through. But you could also interpret that experience in a very different way: a magnificent present from the universe, a perfect opportunity to discover yourself, to become aware of your limits and decide what you really want."

Perplexed, he watched Lorne smiling. Such a strange person, so unlike anyone he had ever met. Would there be room for a Lorne among his acquaintances? An encounter between him and someone like Tom was not easily conceivable. But then again, Lorne had surprised him in so many ways – who really knew what would happen?

"Any news about work?" Lorne said.

There was indeed some interesting news in the aftermath of the start-up.

Kohler had returned. He wanted to start a company, not on behalf of Life Technology Ventures, but on his own. Last week, he had offered Tanya and Martin the possibility of joining him. Tanya had refused on the spot. From now on, she wanted to focus entirely on her academic career.

"I told Kohler that I still needed some time to think," Martin sighed. "It's not easy for me to start over again, you know. With all that happened. But I like Kohler … and he has lots of experience."

"You're close to making a decision, I can hear."

"I guess I am."

They stood up and walked back to the terrace.

As Martin drove down the road towards the motorway, one of Tom's outlandish proverbs appeared in his mind.

When everything starts coming your way, chances are that you have taken the wrong lane.

A twinkle from the past, open to renewed interpretation.

With a little smile, he thought of Sarah who was expecting a well-deserved quiet evening on the couch with a large cup of steaming-hot tea and perhaps a good film on television.

There would be a small change of plan. The time had come to invite her for another walk along those old cobblestones in front of the cathedral.

And for a question that he so fervently wanted to ask.

I would like to express my special gratitude to Virginia Williams for keeping me focused on the pursuit of my dreams, to David Alcorn for his perceptive thoroughness in revising the manuscript and to my wife, Arielle, for her love and inspiring thoughts.

Many other people have been involved with this project in one way or another. I would like to thank them all for their support and encouragement.